About the Auth

Jan_ London and continues to live in the south of the United Kingdom to this present day. He enjoyed reading all kinds of various literature whilst growing up, but in particular gamebooks and other interactive fiction.

His passion for gamebooks would reignite in the mid-2010s through being a member of numerous related groups and communities that are active on social media. Being a part of these would introduce him to others who would go on to become some of his close friends in real life. After a few of them would progress to write their own gamebooks, this inspired him to have a go himself and what you are currently holding is the result of a year's commitment and dedication.

The Fighting Fantasy gamebooks are his favourite series of all time, where he has been both a videographer and volunteer at the fests that have taken place in London since 2014. In addition to this, he has also helped to organise the "You Are The Beer-o" pub quiz events that occur the night before a Fighting Fantasy Fest.

As well as Fighting Fantasy, he is also a massive fan of the TV programme Knightmare, which ran from 1987 to 1994. In 2012 he made a YouTube documentary to commemorate the show's 25th anniversary.

Quadportal is his very first gamebook to be self-published in a physical book format.

QUADPORTAL
Text copyright © 2024 James Aukett
All Rights Reserved

Cover and filler illustrations by Waclaw Traier:
droned.eu
warclawgames.com

Adventure front page illustrations by Matthew Dewhurst

Thanks also to Mark Lain and Victor Cheng
for their invaluable assistance with this book

QUADPORTAL

Four short adventure gamebooks:

- Ripper Reaperman
- Ultraviolator Underworld
- Spiritual Sacrilege
- Tormentor Treetower

Written by James Aukett

CONTENTS

- Welcome!
- Characteristics
- Fighting Battles
- Starting Equipment

- Ripper Reaperman
- Ultraviolator Underworld
- Spiritual Sacrilege
- Tormentor Treetower

- Epilogue
- What Next?
- Other Gamebook Series
- Adventure Sheets

For Em, Helen, Jam and Malthus

WELCOME!

Quadportal is a collection of four short adventure gamebooks where you are the protagonist in each of them. With normal books, the reader usually reads them direct from beginning to end without continuously jumping back and forth to various parts of the book where instructed. But here, in each of these gamebooks you'll be making the decisions that affect what you do during the course of a particular adventure.

All four adventures in this book are 100 sections long each; the rules, characteristics, process for carrying out combat and starting equipment are the same for all of them no matter which adventure you play.

In order to play any of the adventures in this gamebook, you will need the following:
- A pencil
- An eraser
- Two six-sided dice

Your pencil and eraser will be used to record as well as amend information on the Adventure Sheet. There are four Adventure Sheets which can be found at the end of the book – one sheet spread out over two pages per adventure.

The dice will be called to action many times; either as a check against your characteristics or to dictate the unfolding of combat when you come across enemies that you may have to fight. Both your characteristics and the process of how combat works shall be explained over the next few pages.

Whilst playing any of the adventures, there are various routes you can take which may ultimately lead to you either succeeding triumphantly or failing miserably in that particular adventure.

You might be wondering what each adventure entails prior to getting your teeth into a certain one which you decide to undertake? And of course, it is indeed worth outlining what you may possibly find yourself up against. Here's a brief synopsis for all four of the adventures featured:

In **Ripper Reaperman**, your mission will be to explore the streets of Belveslade and find out who is the serial killer that's slaughtering the innocent victims of this town. Can you work out their identity before they get the chance to put an end to your own life?

Then there's **Ultraviolator Underworld**, where you'll going into the Ordno Mines to locate its despised master whose tyranny brings nothing but misery to the long-suffering residents that live in the neighbouring village of Mottinghurst. Are you able to work your way through the tunnels within the mines and deliver justice?

Northgate Abbey is the setting for **Spiritual Sacrilege**, which has experienced the misfortune of a dark priest trespassing into their premises and who's now determined to make it his place to carry out all kinds of tainted necromancy. Will you be the one to aid the noble monks so that a balance of righteousness can be restored to the holy abbey?

And finally, dare you explore **Tormentor Treetower** - working your way up its levels towards the treetower's wicked ruler who is deemed to be a threat beyond the greenery that is Falconleas Wood; only you have the capability to stop him!

With all that in mind, the time has come to prepare yourself for the perils which you might face. Continue over on to the next page and get yourself ready for the challenges you're set to endure…

CHARACTERISTICS

You have four characteristics that will impact how you play each adventure. All four adventures in this book use the same characteristics which are described below:

- BRUTALITY indicates how strong you are and capable of dealing with combat.
- PHYSICALITY is your ability to be agile and fast when up against certain situations.
- MENTALITY gives an understanding of the way your brain responds should you come in any danger as well as your knowledge to solve puzzles and riddles.
- VITALITY is the characteristic that will change the most during any adventure. It shows the level of energy you have within your body and how much health is remaining This score will go up when you eat or drink but also go down if you sustain damage. In the event that your VITALITY reaches zero or below, this means you are dead and must start an adventure all over again.

Now you know what each characteristic entails, the next thing to do is work out the starting scores for each of your characteristics prior to undergoing the adventure you choose to take on:

BRUTALITY: Roll one six-sided die and add 4 to the number rolled. This will give you a starting score of between 5 and 10.

VITALITY: Roll two six-sided dice and add 8 to the number rolled. This gives you a starting score of between 10 and 20.

PHYSICALITY and MENTALITY are worked out differently from your other two characteristics.

You have 15 points which you can allocate between the starting scores for these as you wish. As an example, if you decide that you would like the starting score of your PHYSICALITY to be 8 this means your MENTALITY starting score will be 7.

Note that neither of these characteristics may have a starting score of higher than 10 or lower than 5 (so should it be that your PHYSICALITY has a starting score of 10, the starting score of your MENTALITY will be 5).

Also, as each adventure in this book is stand-alone this means that you cannot carry any of these scores from one adventure into the next. Therefore, if you decide to play another adventure you will need to work out your starting scores for each characteristic all over again.

One final point to take into consideration is that whilst the scores of each of your characteristics will go up and down during an adventure, at no time may they go above your starting scores unless it happens to be stated otherwise.

When you have worked out your starting scores, make a note for each characteristic on the relevant Adventure Sheet at the back of this book.

FIGHTING BATTLES

There will be some occasions where you have an encounter that breaks out into combat. Should such a combat occur, then this will always be a fight to the death with neither yourself or your opponent permitted to escape for the duration of the combat. Begin by making a note of your opponent's BRUTALITY and VITALITY scores in one of the Battle Encounter boxes on the Adventure Sheet that you are using. Then carry out the procedure of combat as follows:

1. Roll two dice and add the total to your BRUTALITY score. This is your Attack Rating.
2. Now roll two dice again and add the total to your opponent's BRUTALITY score. This is their Attack Rating.
3. If you have the higher Attack Rating then you have successfully wounded your opponent, causing them to lose 2 VITALITY points.
4. If your opponent has the higher Attack Rating then they have wounded you, and as a consequence you must deduct 2 points from your VITALITY.
5. If you and your opponent both have the exact same Attack Rating then your blows have glanced off each other, with neither of you sustaining any damage.
6. Repeat the above steps until either you or your opponent's VITALITY drops down to zero.

If your opponent's VITALITY reaches zero first, this means you have won and will be instructed on what to do next.

However, should your VITALITY reach zero then your opponent has killed you and there is no choice but to end the adventure you're currently playing and start all over again.

STARTING EQUIPMENT

You commence each adventure with a few items that will help you along the way. Note that you'll always start with these items regardless of which adventure you're playing:

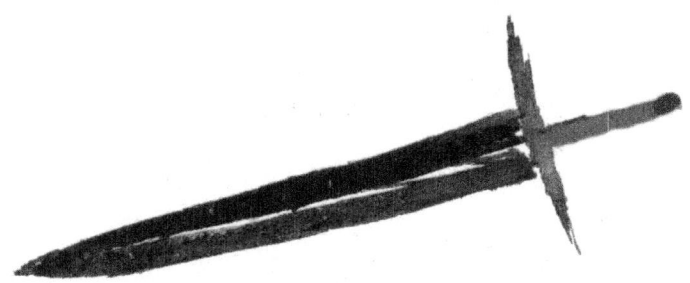

- Sword – this trusty weapon of yours is held inside a scabbard attached to your belt, for easy access when you need to do battle.

- A backpack – to hold any objects you may pick up whilst undergoing your adventure.

- Food Parcels – you'll always begin with three parcels and can eat one of them at any time during the adventure except whilst undertaking combat; doing so will restore up to 4 lost VITALITY points. Each Adventure Sheet has a dedicated space for food parcels; when you do eat one make sure you cross off a relevant box in this section.

**That is all that is needed to be known.
You can now embark on any of the featured adventures.
Good luck and may fortune be with you…**

RIPPER REAPERMAN

Introduction

As night descends on the quiet village of Locksmead, you walk into the establishment known as The Black Horse where a bearded gentleman at the far end acknowledges your presence and states that you have arrived earlier than anticipated. Nevertheless, he directs you to a room located above a flight of stairs and you make your way upwards.

It is a short ascent up the creaking stairs and after searching the narrow passage of the top floor you find that the room you're looking for is tucked away towards the back reaches of the inn. When approaching the room, you knock gently on its sturdy wooden door and a voice from inside responds with one simple word: "Come!"

Opening the door, you walk into the small but extravagantly decorated room with a glistening diamond chandelier hanging from the ceiling and elaborately framed artworks in all their painted glory attached to the walls. A man wearing robes of the finest silks is sat at one end of a table with another chair located at the opposite side. He gestures for you to make yourself comfortable in the vacant seat.

"Thank you for accepting my request of your services", he says, attempting to remain as calm as possible. "Of course, you may be wondering about me and why I have asked you to come here. I am the Marquis of Belveslade which is the adjoining town north of this village. A few nights ago, we lost another innocent victim to a serial killer identifying himself as the Reaper Man. It is the latest in a long line of ripper-like murders committed by this atrocious individual; both myself and my fellow leaders have decided that they must be stopped before they can strike again."

Deliberating briefly over the situation that has just been described, you then ask the Marquis if any potential clues have been gathered that may possibly help to uncover the Reaper Man's identity.

"Alas not", replies the Marquis. "Various hunters in Belveslade have attempted to work out who the person in question could be, but so far none of them have been anywhere near successful in their attempts to do so. This is why I am especially keen to utilise your expertise, for you have a reputation like no other when it comes to locating the offscourings of society such as the one we find ourselves presently up against. It will gratify me immensely to see whoever is responsible face justice and serve the punishment worthy of the horrific crimes they have inflicted upon my beloved town."

It does not take much more convincing before you nod and agree to go into Belveslade so that you can try and track down the Reaper Man. You become determined to stop him before he has the opportunity to add more unsuspecting and helpless victims to his tally.

"Excellent!" says the Marquis with a faint smile. "Now that night time has fallen, there is the strongest of possibilities that our target has begun once more to roam Belveslade's streets in search of their next prey."

Without wanting to prevent any further delay after hearing that particular sentence, you inform the Marquis that you shall waste no more time and set out immediately. Heading back down the stairs, you leave The Black Horse and proceed to make the journey north.

Now turn to **1**

1

Before you are able to commence setting off along the path that leads to Belveslade, the Marquis rushes out with a small cloth pouch which he gives to you.

"As much as I admire your enthusiasm, at least allow me to provide something which may be of assistance!" he insists. Opening the pouch, you find that it contains 10 gold pieces. The bearded gentleman who greeted you in The Black Horse also makes his way outside and once he has approached you, provides three portions of sandwiches to eat during your adventure (make a note of the gold pieces, the sandwiches count as your food parcels).

You thank them both as they wish you the very best of luck. Now is the time to proceed with the walk towards Belveslade. The journey from Locksmead is entirely uneventful as you tread the direct but firm earthen path, finally reaching your intended destination in as little as an hour. Upon arriving at the outskirts, you examine a map pinned to a noticeboard and learn that going straight ahead via Torrens Street leads into the heart of the town square. Despite the ominous warnings of the Reaper Man being at large, you carry on walking and get there without any potential threat of an unwelcome encounter.

Arriving at the town square, you are surprised at the number of places here which are open for trade. Belveslade most definitely has quite the active nightlife even with a ripper or serial killer lurking nearby.

Looking around, you are able to identify a few buildings that could either lead to some vital information relating to the Reaper Man himself or provide you with useful tools for later on during this particular adventure. Where would you like to investigate first?

The fighting arena.	Turn to **42**
The gambling halls.	Turn to **56**
The tavern.	Turn to **70**

2

You walk into the emporium and are greeted by a bespectacled old man with short brown hair and wearing fairly ragged clothing.

"Welcome. How can I be of service?" he says, giving a smile. You explain that you are on the lookout for the Reaper Man that has been terrorising Belveslade and intend to put an end to their ways before any more harm can be inflicted upon by their character. The trader furrows his eyebrows whilst pondering if he might have anything useful within his store. "Hmmm yes, it has sadly become common knowledge that he has made a nuisance of himself around here. I may have some items which may be of good to you – though as can be seen, it might take me a while to find the exact items that I'm thinking of!" is the trader's reply as he starts to rummage through some cluttered shelves.

If you wait and see what the trader comes up with, turn to **16**
If you're in a rush and decide to walk out instead, turn to **40**

3

Led to the very end of the arcade, the curator points to an article on a table and invites you to have a read of its content. Walking up to where it's located, you see that the article is titled Document Three with the subheading *Post Future Recordings* underneath. Although there is no indication of when this was written, it begins with a summary of how the rise of the ancients commenced an era which deeply affected these fabled lands. It goes on to say how destiny's role played an ace to save people from the threat of falling under control to the savage realms. All of a sudden, you then hear a cluster of echoes produced from voices either side of the arcade; concluding that you have spent enough time reading, the urgency of your mission comes back into your thoughts along with the need of pressing on with exactly what it is you are assigned to do.
Turn to **59**

4

You have gained the initiative as you bring Zumbalt's hand closer down to the table. The strongman is not done yet though and he is determined to fight back. Commence another round of combat, noting the decrease in Zumbalt's value due to the current situation being in your favour:

ZUMBALT
BRUTALITY 7

If you and Zumbalt's Attack Ratings are the same, repeat the above process until you both have different scores.
If you have the higher Attack Rating, turn to **11**
If Zumbalt has the higher Attack Rating, turn to **28**

5

Not discouraged by their threats, you stride confidently over to the large table where the three goons are standing.
"You've got a nerve, stranger!" scowls the central goon who taunted you previously.
"What makes you think you have the right to join us?" adds the goon on the left, a man of similar muscular build though sporting a thick brown moustache.
"I'd leave us be right now, for your own sake!" adds the goon on the right with his long, grey beyond shoulder-length hair.
Still refusing to be intimidated, you ask them if they know anything of the Reaper Man.
"And you reckon that we'd tell you anything we've come across? Really, you're more ridiculous that we initially thought. Get out of here before we make this a regrettable encounter for you!" sneers the goon in the centre.
If you decide to punch out at the goons so that they could possibly be taught a lesson, turn to **69**
If you think you can possibly bribe them with money in order for them to part with whatever information they may have, turn to **78**

6

You raise your hands and walk towards the man whilst his pistol is still aimed at you. When you are within an inch of where he stands, the man tells you to follow him. As you are taken down the vennel where he first appeared, you are then instructed to go through a side door. Entering a darkened barely lit room with minimal furnishings, your captor then walks in after you before closing the door and eventually lowering his pistol.
"Apologies for the initially hostile reaction", says the man in a calm, relaxed tone. "I have been informed that you are in search of Belveslade's notorious Reaper Man. If that is indeed the case, could you confirm?" You nod your head in agreement.
"Very pleased to hear it", continues the man. "I am this town's most acclaimed hunter, Barr. It may be of substantial interest to learn about my own fact-finding that I've been undertaking on this ripper in an attempt to locate his whereabouts. This research has been of somewhat mixed results, to say the least. A source of recent discovery provided valuable information that the one we're seeking goes by the name of Walkirsch, though the exact location of where he might reside has so far eluded me. Perhaps you might know of something in connection to what I've gathered which could be of great benefit to us?"
Does the name Walkirsch mean anything to you? If so, then you'll know where he is based. Turn to the section which corresponds with his address. If you haven't been able to work out this information, then turn to **99**

7

The prospect of a dual against a fighter who could be of equal calibre is too good an opportunity to resist, and you inform the usher of your desire to engage in combat with whoever this opponent may be.

"If that is your intention, then come this way if you please!" says the usher as he leads you to the arena's battle ring where upon arrival, you notice a well-armoured warrior standing inside there clutching a sword which undoubtedly looks as impressive as yours. Meeting the referee standing outside the ring, the usher informs him that you'd like to fight the champion. The referee then asks you for the five gold pieces which you hand over (deduct this amount from your Adventure Sheet).

"We have a new challenger!" exclaims the referee to a baying crowd situated at a platform looking above the ring. The Combat Champion stands motionless on the other side whilst the referee walks over to you and states that the battle will be determined by swordplay. If either you or the champion give an indication to stop the fight, the referee will halt the battle and declare the other person as the winner. Drawing your sword, you steel yourself as the champion raises theirs and advances towards you:

COMBAT CHAMPION
BRUTALITY 8 VITALITY 10

As the battle goes on, the champion does indeed prove themself to be a very experienced fighter as the mighty blows produced from yours and their swords clash heavily with each other.

If you reduce the Combat Champion's VITALITY to 4 points or less, turn to **33**

If they reduce your VITALITY to 4 points or less though, turn to **96**

8

Pinning the eye brooch to the back of your tunic, the trader explains that it has a special ability to detect any threats which may be creeping up behind you.
If you would like to buy more items, turn back to **16**
If you have bought all that you need, turn instead to **77**

9

"Never seen him and don't want to end up as their next casualty either!" is the butcher's abrupt reply.
If you now decide to buy some of the meat, turn to **25**
If you've had enough of the butcher's arrogance and leave, turn to **71**

10

You walk along the seemingly quiet cobbled road which appears to have a few shadowy but locked doorways as you continue to make your way past. Feeling that something isn't right despite progressing seemingly unhindered, you try to keep your wits about you whilst treading with caution.
If you are wearing a chimera bracelet, turn to **68**
If you are in possession of an eye brooch, turn to **75**
If you have neither of these, turn to **83**

11

With one last push, you slowly bring Zumbalt's hand down until it is firmly on the table. A slight gasp emits from the crowd as you stand up and look at a dumbstruck Zumbalt, who can't believe that he has been defeated. The adjudicator having witnessed your win, then reaches into his pocket.
"Not many people have got the better of Zumbalt in all the years I've been here!" he mutters as he returns the five gold pieces you staked along with an additional ten gold pieces in winnings (add these to your Adventure Sheet). You smile at the adjudicator and Zumbalt before leaving the room.
Turn to **80**

12

The potion consists of a darkened red liquid inside a circular glass vial. It has medicinal properties and will restore your VITALITY back to its starting score when consumed.
To purchase more items from the trader, turn back to **16**
To make an exit having obtained all you need, turn to **77**

13

You recall the name appearing on the envelope and inform Barr that the man you're trying to find could have their home at Parsonage Close. The hunter reveals it's located on the northern edge of Belveslade, and offers to accompany you there. Heading back outside, you let Barr take the lead as you eventually reach Parsonage Close after what feels like a lengthy time walking. As you both approach the thatched house of the person you suspect, you decide to go in to confront them and Barr agrees to fetch for the Marquis. He wishes you the best of luck before setting off. Eventually left to your own devices, you contemplate how to get inside.
If you have a skeleton key, turn to **27**
If not, turn to **45**

14

Walking up to the bar, you hand over a gold piece to the landlord (deduct this from your Adventure Sheet). He pours a flagon of ale before giving the drink to you, insisting that it is brewed using only the finest hops. Taking the flagon, you turn around to see the three goons eyeing you again.
"Listen here, we don't take too kindly to strangers entering the tavern!" snarls the goon in the centre, a balding man of well-built appearance and a deep scar running down his left cheek. The goons either side of him growl in agreement as if to state in unison that they should not indeed be messed with.
If you try to chat with the goons, turn to **5**
If you'd rather approach the lone man in the corner instead, turn to **21**

15

Gizpiel chuckles to himself as he takes away your five gold pieces (deduct these from your Adventure Sheet).
"I don't suppose you'd like to play again?" asks Gizpiel with a smile that looks keen for you to have a second try.
If you have another five gold pieces and wish to stake them, turn to **30**
If not or you would prefer to back out, then turn to **91**

16

The trader eventually finds three items which he believes could be beneficial to you. He places them on a desk and states how much they each cost. Take a look at the items listed below and their price in gold pieces. If you decide to buy any of them, turn to the relevant section to find out what that particular item does:

Eye Brooch	*2 Gold Pieces*	Turn to **8**
Potion of Strength	*5 Gold Pieces*	Turn to **12**
Skeleton Key	*10 Gold Pieces*	Turn to **24**

If you choose not to purchase any of the above, then you apologise to the trader for wasting his time before exiting. Turn to **40**

17

Your blow comes directly into the central goon's nose, sending him reeling on to the floor. Enraged, his two accomplices respond by drawing their weapons to inflict revenge but are suddenly interrupted by a loud *"STOP!"*. The landlord has armed himself with a rifle and is aiming it perfectly towards the scene of the commotion.
"Both of you ought to know better in here!" he says at the two goons still standing.
"And as for you", continues the landlord, slowly turning to point the rifle in your direction. "Get out of this tavern – you're barred!" Placing the flagon of ale on the nearest table, you do as the landlord has instructed and leave quietly. Whilst making your way out, the central goon steadily picks himself up with one hand covering his bloodied nose and mutters some unintelligible curse words towards your way. It is most certainly a fact that you won't be drinking in this tavern ever again should you happen to come back to Belveslade in the weeks or years to come.
Turn to **98**

18

The mirror has the finest and most exquisite platinum decorated around its edges, and engraved into the top is the slogan: *Let it be your time.* As you look through the mirror, your body starts to feel more rejuvenated and eventually you see the reflection of yourself showing a more confident look about you. This particular mirror has enhanced magical powers; you may regain 1 BRUTALITY point if you happened to lose this earlier on during the adventure. Satisfied with the glowing aura produced by the sensation that's just occurred, you decide it's a good idea to now make a departure from the venue on a positive wave of energy that has been initiated by the fascinating buzz you've happened to experience.
Turn to **59**

19

You tell the usher that you would like to take on the strongman and are led to a side room where inside stands an adjudicator standing next to a reinforced metal table. Sitting at one end of this table is a bald moustached man of immensely muscular physique.
"Think you can overcome the mighty Zumbalt in an arm wrestle, eh?" asks the adjudicator, and you give him five gold pieces in response.
"Very well then, take a seat!" is the adjudicator's reaction as he points to a chair at the other side of the table. You sit down, and Zumbalt looks towards you with a menacing glance after you have seated yourself. The adjudicator tells both of you to place your right elbow on the table, then lock hands with each other.
"Whoever forces the other's hand down to the table first is the winner!" emphasises the adjudicator as a small crowd enters the room to witness the contest before them. You and Zumbalt stare into each other's eyes for a fleeting moment before the adjudicator signals for the wrestle to begin. As your own arm pits itself against Zumbalt's, you realise how strong he indeed is. Carry out one round of combat, making a note of Zumbalt's value below:

ZUMBALT
BRUTALITY 8

If you have the higher Attack Rating, turn to **4**
If you and Zumbalt's Attack Ratings are the same, turn to **28**
If Zumbalt has the higher Attack Rating, turn to **55**

20

Watching the butcher carefully as you allow him to get slowly back up on his feet, he regains his breath with your sword raised towards his neck in case there happens to be any unexpected movements.

"Okay, so that mysterious person who was with me a moment ago is known as the Reaper Man", admits the butcher. "Yet I do not know what his real name is. He became aware of what I could do thanks to word of mouth about my profession. Most nights he would bring a freshly murdered victim to me and demand that I cut up the body parts in the dead of night once Belveslade had ceased all its evening activity. If I refused to co-operate, then he would threaten myself and my family with a fate similar to that of his victims. Let me help you put an end to his murderous spree; put down your sword and I will give you the evidence needed that can stop this Reaper Man's foul reign of terror." You nod and lower your sword, then the butcher walks over to a corner of the storeroom where he unlocks a drawer and takes something out. Returning to where you stand, he hands this over and upon taking it you notice it's a book of some kind.

"This log book details each and every transaction I've had with the Reaper Man – all sixty-four of them", says the butcher with remorse. "Now that it is in your possession, I promise to cease trading here. Both myself and my family will move away from Belveslade; this place may soon gain another butcher but hopefully by then the Reaper Man will be no more. I believe that you are the person to put an end to his existence, stranger."

Informing the butcher that if he is not gone within a week, you will tell the Marquis of the dealings with the Reaper Man that have taken place in here. Hastily agreeing to what you've said, the butcher then goes to a pantry in another part of the storeroom and pulls out some dried strips of meat which he offers to you.

"These are my finest cooked pieces of venison!" assures the butcher. Consuming the meat, you do indeed find them rather nourishing; restore 4 VITALITY points. Make a note that you have the log book on your Adventure Sheet. Then reminding the butcher of what you've vowed to do if he hasn't made tracks within a week before you leave, it is time once more to head back outside and continue your pursuit of the Reaper Man.
Turn to **71**

21

Making your way over to the raggedly unkempt man, you ask if you can join him and he nods.
"Yeah, that's right - you two oddballs deserve each other!" mocks the central goon with a heavy laugh, still looking rather shiftily in your direction.
"Ignore him, that guy and his pals are nothing but trouble!" mutters the unkempt man as you sit next to where he is. "Stranger, hope you don't mind if I can ask the following- what brings you to Belveslade?"
If you reply that you're hunting the Reaper Man, turn to **47**
If you say that you just happen to be passing by, turn to **65**

22

Handing a gold piece over to the curator, he then begins to go over the exhibits that are available to you.
"If you like reading, then Document Three could be of interest", he says. "Or maybe you'd like to witness the spectacle inside our theatre? Failing either of those, you can take a look at the Wilderness of Mirrors for a curiously distorted interpretation of the present."
Which of these exhibits appeals the most?
Document Three.	Turn to **3**
The Spectacle.	Turn to **48**
The Wilderness of Mirrors.	Turn to **79**

23

You place five gold pieces on the wooden table then sit yourself down. Gizpiel rolls the two dice first - they land on six and one, comprising a total of seven. He then hands the dice over and instructs you to play. Roll the two dice to see what you come up with!
If you roll less than seven, turn to **15**
If you roll exactly seven, turn to **49**
If you roll more than seven, turn to **67**

24

A glint appears in the trader's eye as he tells you that the skeleton key has the capability to open any unlocked door.
Are you in need of more items? If so, turn back to **16**
All done purchasing what you need? Turn instead to **77**

25

The butcher will sell you a portion of dried beef strips for 1 gold piece. If you buy them, it counts as one food parcel. Make the necessary amendments on your Adventure Sheet if you do purchase the beef. Regardless if you've bought them or not, the time then comes for you to leave the butcher's and continue with your adventure.
Turn to **71**

26

You give Donowen one portion of your sandwiches which they gratefully accept (deduct one food parcel from your Adventure Sheet). After washing them down with some water provided by the medics, Donowen then looks up and speaks to you.

"Not many people are kind to give aid once they've bested me!" they say courteously. Smiling in acknowledgement, you then take the opportunity to ask Donowen if they known anything of the Reaper Man that lurks in Belveslade.

"Well, I've been fortunate not to have been in contact with them - put it that way!" is their response. "If it's a serial killer you're looking for, seek out the trader who resides on Commerce Road. He's bound to have something that will help you track down this ripper. Also, I personally know one of the hunters that's pursuing the same target as yourself. This hunter usually arms themself with a flintlock pistol and should you happen to cross paths, then I suggest treating him with utmost respect. Good luck, proven warrior!"

Thanking Donowen for their information, you turn round to see the referee waiting to return you the five gold pieces you previously wagered plus an extra ten gold pieces in prize money. Add these to your Adventure Sheet before leaving the ring to continue on your way.

Turn to **80**

27

You take out the skeleton key and prepare to insert it inside the lock. Once the key is in, it takes a while before you figure out the best way to turn it which initiates a clicking mechanism that opens the door. Pushing the door to reveal what lies beyond, you see before you an eerie-looking passage. Taking a moment to steady yourself for what could be a showdown with the Reaper Man, you then place the key back in your pocket before entering the house.

Turn to **60**

28

You and Zumbalt happen to be equally matched at present. Commence another round of combat:

ZUMBALT
BRUTALITY 8

If you and Zumbalt's Attack Ratings are the same, repeat the above process until you have different scores.
If you have the higher Attack Rating, turn to **4**
If Zumbalt has the higher Attack Rating, turn to **55**

29

Taking the opportunity to cover your ears with your hands, you soon regain focus and your mind clears to plan an escape past the musicians. Keeping your ears well covered and your eyes open, you dodge round them as they continue to play their ghastly ditty. The musicians do not challenge or confront you as to why you're not stopping to hear the haunting melody from their instruments. When you're at a comfortable distance out of their reach via a street corner, you stop to catch your breath. Having uncovered your ears, the sound from the musicians soon subsides and you feel ready enough to carry on as normal again. Continuing along, you arrive at another junction where you learn that you have reached the opposite of Linzberg Staples. Another path leading off here appears to go back south so you make the decision to head north along Dervish Way.
Turn to **10**

30

You place another five gold pieces on the table and then Gizpiel rolls the two dice again. To everyone's astonishment including your own, they land on two sixes! Knowing that he rolled at least one six last time, you're wondering how he's managing to get a streak of consistent high numbers. Roll two dice to deal with a separate matter on this occasion.
If it's less than or equal to your MENTALITY, turn to **62**
If the result is greater than your MENTALITY, turn to **89**

31

The very instant he sees you reach for your sword, the man fires his pistol which shoots a bullet that lodges into your heart within seconds. You die immediately from the effect of the bullet and fall to the ground. It definitely wasn't a good idea to challenge one of Belveslade's most skilled hunters when they're certain to have a very accurate shot on target. Your adventure ends here.

32

Having spent a few moments scratching his jaw, the central goon eventually decides to accept your offer and then takes the gold pieces from the table (deduct the relevant amount from your Adventure Sheet). He then beckons you to one side of the tavern, and you go to hear what he has to say.
"Normally we don't help strangers so I'm only going to tell you once!" he insists. "Us three have never met this so-called Reaper Man, and for his sake we hope it stays like that. Another regular who frequents this establishment though recently informed us that this character has been spotted engaging in some transactions with the butcher who plies his business on Viamultain Avenue. Now I suggest you clear off before we get fed up of your ugly mug!"
Acting on the central goon's last words, you do as instructed and make your way out of the tavern without hesitation.
Turn to **98**

33

Your sword lands a deep blow on the champion, who screams then raises a hand to draw attention to their injury. The referee enters the ring to declare you the winner, which results in a surprised and muted applause from the crowd. Two medics then appear to treat the champion's wound. As they are getting bandaged, the champion removes their helmet and you discover that you have been fighting against a woman with short brown wavy hair.

"Well done warrior, that was one of the hardest battles I've fought in this arena!" they acknowledge towards you. "My name is Donowen and not many people have got the better of me in combat, let me tell you!"

If you wish to speak to Donowen further, turn to **51**
If you'd rather just claim your winner's prize, turn to **72**

34

Walking into the butchers, you notice that the shelves and racks are completely empty with the exception of some meat located behind a glass counter. The butcher himself is nowhere to be seen, so you give a slight cough in an attempt to get a reaction.

"I'll be with you in a minute!" is the loud response from an ajar doorway situated to the side of the counter.

If you wait as the butcher instructs, turn to **57**
If you walk through the doorway to find out what he's doing, turn to **88**

35

You manage to jump carefully over the wide spreading liquid which continues to spill in the opposite direction from where you now stand. Looking ahead, you see that the shadowy figure has sprinted off into the distance so you run in order to catch up with him. Turning round a corner before arriving at another junction however, you pause to look around but the figure is nowhere to be seen. As you take another moment to work out where you are, you notice that you are now at the other end of Linzberg Staples with another street leading off from this junction also appearing to eventually lead back south. Therefore, you make the decision to head north along Dervish Way.
Turn to **10**

36

A gasp erupts as you match Gizpiel's score. You take your five gold pieces off the table and reclaim them as yours. Some whispering and faint murmurs start to take place between the punters and even Gizpiel doesn't look too happy either, but you think to yourself that none of this should concern you. Not wanting to waste any more time here, you take your leave of Gizpiel and the others.
Turn to **91**

37

"Well given that this is the austerity exhibition and aims to show favour towards those less fortunate, I'll let you see any exhibit free of charge!" says the curator encouragingly. You thank him as he begins to inform you of the exhibits currently available, and it could well indeed be worthwhile to have a close look at what is on offer. Choose which of the following interests you the most:

Document Three.	Turn to **3**
The Spectacle.	Turn to **48**
The Wilderness of Mirrors.	Turn to **79**

38

You run your sword against the butcher's throat and look down as he spends his dying moments bleeding on the ground. That figure he was dealing with could have well been the one you're seeking; if the butcher was indeed aiding and abetting the Reaper Man's crimes then you deem it only right to have delivered the justice he deserves. Examining the storeroom afterwards, you notice that it is almost as empty as what you saw when you walked in. The meat you do see appears too raw to eat, and so you head back out of the butchers to track down that mysterious person.
Turn to **71**

39

At last, the door smashes open. Hinges come loose from the fixings they were attached to and you push the door aside, walking through the passage to investigate the house.
Turn to **60**

40

Leaving the emporium behind, you continue onwards and soon turn right into Threnode Crescent. There is an eerie aura felt in the air as you continue onwards, and soon you face three pale characters awkwardly playing some musical instruments. Examining them from left to right, you see the leftmost individual plucking deeply low notes from an acoustic guitar. The performer in the centre occasionally bangs on a large red drum strapped around their neck, and the fellow on the right blows a mournful melody through a mouth organ. It's a rather disturbing ballad that emits from their collective ensemble, which makes you extremely unsettled. You will have to regain composure if you are to bring yourself together and overcome the musician's haunting symphony. Roll two dice.
If it's less than or equal to your MENTALITY, turn to **29**
If the result is greater than your MENTALITY, turn to **63**

41

The mugger whips out a dagger from his pocket; your response is to draw your own sword for a fight that will ideally stop his thievery:

MUGGER
BRUTALITY 6 VITALITY 6

If you win, turn to **87**

42

At the main door which leads to the fighting arena, you are greeted by an usher who looks up then down at you to examine what's before him from head to toe.

"Welcome. You certainly have the physique of an experienced warrior – I guess you are here to prove yourself in our arena?" asks the usher. "There are two contests that you can participate in; the first is a battle versus our very own hardened combat champion and the second is an arm wrestle against undoubtedly the strongest man in Belveslade. Either contest will cost you five gold pieces should you choose to prove your worth, though of course you will get this back alongside an additional prize sum in the unlikely event you emerge victorious. Please tell me, do either of these contests appeal to you?"

If you want to do battle with the combat champion, turn to **7**
If you're up for a tussle with the strongman, turn to **19**
If you decline to take part in both contests, turn to **80**

43

There is a click from a mechanism in the armchair which releases a dart that shoots out towards you're standing. However, your reactions are fast enough to allow you to speedily jump to one side. The dart misses, thudding into the wall behind. As you turn to look in the direction of the Reaper Man, you watch him furiously grab a knife from a nearby rack then rush at you enragedly screaming. Unsheathing your sword, you get ready to defend yourself in a fight to the death:

REAPER MAN
BRUTALITY 8 VITALITY 8

If you win, turn to **100**

44

Heading over to the dice table, you are greeted by a swathe of fellow punters standing over another man who's sitting and looking rather sinewy in his appearance with a brown ragged beard. This man, having seen you make your way to the table, moves two dice around in the palm of his hand and invites you to play a game.
"My name is Gizpiel - how lucky are you feeling?" the man asks. "Five gold pieces and you can find out if the dice are in your favour!"
If you stake the requested five gold pieces, turn to **23**
If you decide against playing and make an exit, turn to **91**

45

You have no option but to try and break down the sturdy wooden door. Taking a few steps backwards and drawing in all of your strength, you then charge at it with your shoulder. Roll two dice.
If it's less than or equal to your BRUTALITY, turn to **52**
If the result is greater than your BRUTALITY, turn to **73**

46
You cannot withstand Zumbalt's might any longer as he forces your hand down to the table. Once he finally lets go, you find your hand throbbing in pain; lose 1 BRUTALITY and 2 VITALITY points. Barely having time to recover, the adjudicator then requests that you leave the room which you do to a series of jeers and heckles from the crowd.
Turn to **80**

47
You boldly state that you intend to seek out and stop the Reaper Man from continuing his recent spree of killing.
"Aye, I've heard that he's malicious and good at covering his tracks!" replies the unkempt man. "But I tend to stay here in the warm safety, thankful that I have yet to encounter him. If this ripper is as bloodthirsty as many have claimed him to be, then you'll need some protection along your way."
Pulling a bracelet off his wrist, the man hands it over to you and instructs to put it on. Doing so, you then notice that it has the symbol of a chimera embossed on to it. Thanking him for his gift, you let the man have the rest of your ale in return. (Note down that you have the chimera bracelet.)
You then get up and leave the tavern without even looking at the goons on the other table who had previously taunted you.
Turn to **98**

48

The curator takes you through a corridor past the left of the arcade, where at the end is situated the venue's theatre. Before going in, you peak through an ossirian window next to the point of entry; it doesn't look like there are many other people in attendance. Walking past where you are standing, the curator then waits patiently as you eventually make your way inside.

"Make yourself comfortable, for the show is about to get underway!" he insists as you take a seat at the back. Half an hour or so passes by as you watch a giant spectral hand controlling a skeletal jester puppet on the stage. The spectacle is interesting to watch even if it doesn't provide you with any clues in regards to your mission. But you do take advantage of some complimentary cheese and wine that is offered to you during the performance; restore 4 VITALITY points if previously wounded. Once everything has drawn to a close, the pressing matter of tracking down the Reaper Man occurs in your thoughts. Not wanting to lose any more precious time, you rise from your seat and briefly regather your belongings as you head out of the theatre focused on recommencing pursuit of the very man himself.
Turn to **59**

49

A puzzled look appears on Gizpiel's face, but he allows you to claim back the five gold pieces you staked.

"Why not re-stake those gold pieces and play again?" asks Gizpiel, albeit in a more serious tone.

If you put the five gold pieces back on the table, turn to **30**
If you refuse and walk away instead, turn to **91**

50

You reach the end of Dervish Way without any further incident and emerge into another square area. Looking around, all you see is houses on each side with a few vennels situated in between some of them. Whilst wondering where to go from here, a man emerges from the vennel directly ahead. He has a beard with his hair tied into a bun, though you are more concerned by the huge flintlock pistol he is aiming towards you.

"Now then, you're coming with me!" says the man as he continues to advance forward. "Don't even think about doing any sudden movements or tricks – just comply with my instructions and everything will be okay, you understand?" This man is extremely serious and looks like he's not to be reckoned with! How do you respond?

Approach the man as he requests?	Turn to **6**
Draw your sword to attack?	Turn to **31**
Spin round and make a run for it?	Turn to **92**

51

Impressed by how graceful and humble Donowen is in defeat, you feel that some beneficial assistance could be earned here if you can manage to persuade them in some fitting way or another.

They may appreciate something to eat that could help recover some of their strength. Should you wish to offer one of your food parcels, then turn to **26**

If you would rather try speaking to them without doing this, turn to **93**

52

The door splinters as you smash through it, causing the hinges on the opposite side of the lock to come off completely. You are now free to walk through the passage leading inside.

Turn to **60**

53

Roll one die.
If the number rolled is less than or equal to the number of gold pieces you've offered the goons, turn to **32**
If the number is greater than the amount of gold pieces you're willing to part with, turn to **86**

54

Walking into the venue, you emerge into a dingily lit arcade. A man has seen you enter and proceeds to walk to where you're standing. He is small and old, though very smartly dressed with a well-groomed appearance complimented by an endearing smile.

"Greetings, I am the curator. You are here for the exhibition, I assume?" he enquires. "There are a number of fascinating exhibits on at present, with each of them costing one gold piece in order to have a leisurely perusal into whatever it is they may entail."

If you have a gold piece, turn to **22**
If not, turn to **37**

55

Zumbalt has the initiative! Growing in strength, he is on the verge of pinning your hand to the table as you desperately summon all of your willpower to try and get back on level terms. Commence another round of combat, though you must note the increase in Zumbalt's value due to his current advantage:

ZUMBALT
BRUTALITY 9

If you and Zumbalt's Attack Ratings are the same, repeat the above process until you both have different scores.
If you have the higher Attack Rating, turn to **28**
If Zumbalt has the higher Attack Rating, turn to **46**

56

You head into the gambling halls and once you're beyond the entrance, are met by a clerk situated at a desk. Approaching him, he begins to speak whilst you listen to what exactly it is he has to say.

"The halls are very busy this evening!" insists the clerk. "A large number of private parties have booked up much of what is available. Only game that's currently allowing new participants is dice, otherwise you'll have to come back when we're not as crowded!"

Acknowledging his words, what would you like to do?

Pay a visit to the dice table.   Turn to **44**
Make your way out and look elsewhere.   Turn to **91**

57

Eventually the butcher comes to make himself known and proceeds to look at you with a suspicious glance from the other side of the counter.

"Well... what can I do for you?" he demands impatiently.

If you ask if he knows anything relating to the Reaper Man, turn to **9**

If you would like to buy some meat, turn to **25**

58

Commerce Road is Belveslade's main shopping precinct where both locals and visitors can browse its shops which are host to many weird and wonderful artefacts. Some of the heirlooms that can be obtained from these parts are one of a kind, highly valued relics. However, it is now rather late in the evening and many of the shops have closed for the day. Despite this, you do find one displaying an open sign; it is interestingly named Traill's Emporium and has a few unusual items situated on various shelves stacked behind its front window.

If you're curious to see what's available inside, turn to **2**

If you'd rather keep on walking past, turn to **40**

59

You leave the venue by the same way you entered, with the curator standing by the door as you do so.
"Thank you for visiting the exhibition – do come again!" he says warmly as you find yourself back outside and proceed to carry on down Linzberg Staples once more.
Turn to **97**

60

A few metres along the passage, you come across a living room to the left. Stepping inside to find out what is within, you instantly find yourself face to face with a man seated in an armchair. He is not old but does have long, grey hair with a goatee beard and is wearing thin round glasses. Dressed from the shoulders down all in black, the man looks somewhat perturbed that you have entered his residence without any sort of warranted invitation.
"What are you doing here and why have you interrupted my plans during this night time?" he demands. You cut straight to the chase and ask if his name is Walkirsch.
"And if it is, of what concern does it matter to you?" is his more agitated reply. Needing no further prompting given his haughty attitude, you state that you believe him to be the serial killer known as the Reaper Man.
"Oh, is that so? Tell me then, you've broke into my property illegally and now you're making this preposterous accusation that I am a murderer of numerous hapless victims – can you prove that I am who you are claiming to be with such documentation known as evidence?" Pausing for a brief second, you realise that you will indeed have to verify everything you've said. If you do have an item that links the accused to their crimes, you will know how many transactions were recorded in it. Turn immediately to the section which corresponds with this number of transactions. If you don't have this or have forgotten the exact number, then you must turn to **94**

61

The butcher drops his cleaver to the ground and crouches down, begging for mercy.
"Please spare my menial life, I'll reveal everything there is to know!" he sobs. How will you address the situation?
If you agree to show mercy to him, turn to **20**
If you slay the butcher for what he's done, turn to **38**

62

Noticing that one of the dice is almost on the edge of the table, you peer underneath to see that Gizpiel is holding a magnet in his other hand. The man is cheating by using a loaded die! You think fast enough to swipe the magnet out of his hand and whilst Gizpiel reacts alarmed at what you're doing, you show the magnet to the other punters who become as equally shocked.
"I always knew you were a cheat, Gizpiel!" snarls one of them as they begin to turn their attention on the fraudster. Panicking, Gizpiel is helpless as he becomes outnumbered by the angry mob. Removing your five gold pieces from the table, one of the other punters then turns around to face you.
"Thanks for proving what a weasel he is – here's a small reward in appreciation!" nods the other punter as he hands you an extra ten gold pieces. With a grateful smile, you leave Gizpiel to receive the comeuppance he rightfully deserves.
Turn to **91**

63

The musician's wailing harmonies causes you to lose all concentration. Desperate to put a stop to this as soon as possible, you quickly retreat. Running back down Commerce Road, you soon find yourself back at the junction. Not wanting to encounter them again, you decide to opt for a different route.
To head north via Linzberg Staples, turn to **76**
To go east along Viamultain Avenue, turn to **95**

64

You pull out the log book and advise him that you're aware of every dealing he's had with the butcher. Walkirsch initially begins to panic, and shakily reaches down for a hidden compartment in his armchair. Having watched his every move, you are prepared to avoid whatever he may be releasing. Roll two dice.
If it's less than or equal to your PHYSICALITY, turn to **43**
If the total is greater than your PHYSICALITY, turn to **81**

65

The unkempt man erupts into a howl of deranged laughter.
"No fool in their right mind would come here without a valid reason, especially when there's a serial killer wandering at large!" he taunts. "And people say *I'm* the one who is mad in this forsaken place!"
Having overheard this conversation, the goons then join in with the heckling. Feeling slightly embarrassed, you decide to make a swift exit from the tavern before the situation can get any worse.
Turn to **98**

66

You look at the mirror which has a pile of mounting ashes at the bottom. Whilst staring at it in a mindset of curiosity, the image displayed by the mirror warps so that instead of your own reflection you are aghast to be confronted by a pair of flesh ghosts who reach out of the mirror to feast on your soul. Fortunately, you retreat backwards before you can be fully consumed by them. Despite avoiding the worst that could have happened, the horrific experience has still weakened you severely. Your current VITALITY score is halved (rounding any fractions down). Getting away from the mirrors to avoid sustaining any more damage, there is an urgency within you to escape the venue altogether.
Turn to **59**

67

The punters surrounding Gizpiel cheer when you land the higher score. Not too happy about this himself, Gizpiel pulls out five gold pieces from his pocket which he gives to you in addition to the other five that you staked.

"Beginner's luck!" moans Gizpiel. "Perhaps you should play again if you're feeling more confident!" Do you reckon that fortune will be siding with you for a second time?

If you stake another five gold pieces, turn to **30**
If you decide to quit whilst you're ahead, turn to **91**

68

As you walk along, you suddenly feel the sensation of your wrist tingling where your bracelet is. Taking a moment to stop and examine what's going on, you turn around and come face to face with a scrawny young man attempting to reach for one of your pockets. He's clearly trying to rob you!
Turn to **41**

69

That does it. You've had enough of the bad-mannered attitude from the goons and lash out towards their way with your fist in order to teach them a lesson. Roll two dice.
If it's less than or equal to your PHYSICALITY, turn to **17**
If the total is greater than your PHYSICALITY, turn to **82**

70

Entering a tavern named "The Head of the Serpent", you find that it's not too busy this evening. A scruffy-looking man sits by himself in one corner appearing to be content, whilst three menacing gentlemen at another table eye you suspiciously. The landlord at the bar also looks towards you.
"The finest ale in all of Belveslade! A pint for just one gold piece!" shouts the landlord in your direction.
If you would like to purchase a drink, turn to **14**
If you decline the price and leave, turn to **98**

71

It is not long before you are well away from the butchers and turning left into Murphyjohn Lane. As you continue forwards, you then happen to espy a shadowy figure standing next to a large canister. They are wearing a stovepipe hat and donning a long black cloak that covers most of their features. Could this be… ?

You have no time to think any further as the figure kicks the canister towards your direction which tips on to the ground and releases a hissing green-coloured liquid. The fumes emitting from this substance cause you to cover your nose and mouth with your hand, such is the unpleasant foul odour. As the liquid advances near the spot where you're standing, you desperately try to ensure it doesn't come into contact with you whilst the figure ahead makes a prompt getaway. Roll two dice.

If it's less than or equal to your PHYSICALITY, turn to **35**

If the total is greater than your PHYSICALITY, turn to **90**

72

You nod towards Donowen in recognition of their gratitude. The referee returns the five gold pieces you wagered before commencing battle, plus an additional ten gold pieces for your victory (make the necessary adjustments on your Adventure Sheet). Very pleased with your gains, the important matter of the main mission returns to your mind and so you decide to move on.
Turn to **80**

73

Despite your best efforts, the door stays firmly resistant and you end up having to momentarily nurse a bruised shoulder. Lose 2 VITALITY points. Resting briefly, you regain courage and make another attempt to smash down the door. Roll two dice again.
If it's less than or equal to your BRUTALITY, turn to **39**
If the total is greater than your BRUTALITY, turn to **85**

74

With a look of dejection, you cannot prevent Gizpiel taking your five gold pieces (deduct these from your Adventure Sheet). Concluding that your adventure should be of more pressing concern, you stand up and make your way out.
"Do come again, it's been a pleasure to play with you!" says Gizpiel with a delighted mocking laugh as you exit with a sense of melancholy.
Turn to **91**

75

Your tunic begins to feel heavy where the brooch has been attached, then you remember the words of the trader. Spinning round, your eyes directly meet those of a scrawny young man with one of his arms reached out in an attempt to relieve you of your possessions!
Turn to **41**

76

Linzberg Staples feels almost derelict as you walk along, with buildings either having their windows covered by wooden panels or doors secured by long nailed planks. One particular building looks to be open however and its appearance catches your attention. Its façade is painted entirely in black and white, and you guess that it is some sort of concert hall or theatre. Above the entrance is a sign boldly displaying the name Le Zebre De Belleville, and to the side is a board with the somewhat crudely painted words on it: The Austerity Exhibition – Now Open. Glimpsing through, the door is open should you wish to go inside.
If you decide to have a look, turn to **54**
If you ignore it and continue past, turn to **97**

77

Thanking the trader for the items he has provided you with, the time comes to head back out and continue with your primary objective. But at least there is a satisfactory feeling within you that you're now better equipped to deal with this. "Good luck in tracking down the Reaper Man!" says the trader as you reply with a farewell.
Turn to **40**

78

You reach into your pocket to grab a handful of gold pieces and place them on the table where the goons are standing. Mentioning that you'd be willing to pay them for any information they may know in relation to the Reaper Man, the goons look down at the gold pieces whilst contemplating your offer. They seem a tad hesitant at whether they should actually be helping you judging by the reactions they're giving off, but nonetheless are still giving the prospect at earning a bit of extra money some thought. Decide how many gold pieces you would like to bribe the goons with, then turn to **53**

79

Following the curator as he leads you through to the right of the arcade, you then enter a doorway and head past a foldable screen. Located here are the mirrors of this exhibition. Taking some time to have a close look at each of them, all of the various mirrors show twisted reflections of yourself before two larger freestanding mirrors catch your attention. Placed side by side next to each other, which of them do you want to examine in detail?
To have a look at the mirror on the left, turn to **18**
To have a look at the mirror on the right, turn to **66**

80

Proceeding to leave the fighting arena via the same door you entered, the usher who initially greeted you bids a good evening as you leave quietly. Now provided you haven't already been to them, there is still an opportunity to visit either of the following:

The gambling halls.	Turn to **56**
The tavern.	Turn to **70**

If you're ready to continue elsewhere on your adventure, turn to **84**

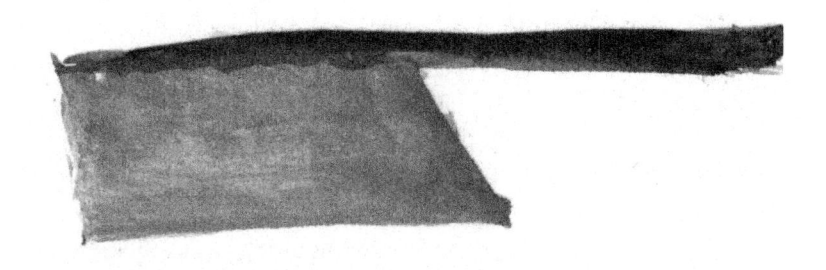

81

A dart fires out from the armchair's hidden compartment with a whoosh and you promptly realise that it targeted where you stand. Desperately, you try to jump out of the way. However, you're not swift enough to prevent the dart from clipping the side of your elbow. The dart was tipped with poison and in seconds, you begin to feel the unfortunate harmful side effects; roll one die and lose that many VITALITY points. If you're still alive, you recover to see the Reaper Man grab a large knife from a metal rack beside his armchair then charge towards you screaming. Pulling out your own sword, you've become more determined than ever to end this sadistic psychopath's wiles once and for all:

REAPER MAN
BRUTALITY 8 VITALITY 8

If you win, turn to **100**

82

Aiming for the central goon, your feeble punch misses him. Incensed by this, the other two goons respond by each of them firmly grabbing both your arms and legs before hauling you out of the tavern. Once outside, they then throw you down on to the hard ground and are eventually joined by the central goon who approaches you. Then all three begin a vicious process of repeatedly kicking and stamping on you whilst you lie defenceless, unable to reach for your sword. Then they finally stop, having become satisfied with the bruises they've inflicted on you. The beating you have received is bad enough for you to lose 4 VITALITY points. If you're still alive, you pick yourself up from the ground. "Don't ever let us catch you in here again!" barks the central goon as all three go back inside the tavern to resume their drinking. You decide that it's best not to follow suit.
Turn to **98**

83

Making it to the end of Dervish Way, you're still convinced that nothing is quite what it seems. As you put your hands to your pockets though, your worst suspicions are confirmed. Someone has managed to silently creep up behind you and steal all your money! Cross any gold pieces you may have previously had off your Adventure Sheet. Enraged to have fallen victim to this thievery, there is nothing else you can do but continue onwards.
Turn to **50**

84

You take the only path leading out of the town square which is via White Wall Alley. Not much long afterwards, you arrive at a junction with three different streets leading off from here. Which route do you wish to take?
To proceed west along Commerce Road, turn to **58**
To go north along Linzberg Staples, turn to **76**
To head east along Viamultain Avenue, turn to **95**

85

The door is very rigid and as fiercely strong as you may be, you cannot break down what is before you. Such has been the roughness of this ordeal that in fact, your attempts have resulted in your shoulder feeling extremely sore and painful. As you clutch on to it momentarily, a window of the house you were trying to enter silently opens and seconds later a crossbow bolt flies out into the exact spot where you stand. You are so busy tending to your shoulder that you cannot stop the fast-moving crossbow bolt impaling deep into the lower part of your stomach, which culminates in you slumping downwards to a fate that will undoubtedly be far worse when the Reaper Man gets hold of you. For it was indeed this very person who triggered the lethal shot, and despite you finding his hideaway it is the ripper who has the last laugh. Your adventure ends here.

86

With a joint burst of laughter, the goons mock the measly amount of gold pieces you've placed before them.

"Think you can persuade us with such a pathetic sum?" ridicules the central goon. "Be off with you before things get even worse!" What will you try now?

To talk with the lone man sat in the corner, turn to **21**

If you want to start a fight with the odious goons, turn to **69**

Or to leave the tavern, turn to **98**

87

It is easy to work out why the mugger was so keen to indulge in robbing a wandering passer-by. Searching his pockets, they yield just one silver piece and an envelope addressed to *Walkirsch, 13 Parsonage Close*. The envelope has been opened but examining it you find that it doesn't contain anything. You can take either or both of these items with you before heading onwards.

Turn to **50**

88

Storming past the counter, you push the door open and emerge into the butcher's storeroom. The butcher is here having a discussion with another man wearing a stovepipe hat and a long black cloak. All of a sudden, they notice you and the cloaked figure reacts by running off through another doorway situated at the far end. The butcher grabs hold of a cleaver from the table next to him then charges at you. Drawing your sword, you get ready to defend yourself from the butcher as he swings the cleaver with rage:

BUTCHER
BRUTALITY 7 VITALITY 8

If you manage to reduce the butcher's VITALITY to 2 points or less, turn to **61**

89
You are unable to work out Gizpiel's successful streak, and are left to somehow achieve a miracle. Roll two dice again.
If you also manage to roll twelve, turn to **36**
If you roll anything less than that, turn to **74**

90
You cannot prevent the liquid from touching your boots, which seeps and initiates a painful sensation in your feet. Instantly you realise that the liquid is none other than acid which is making your feet very sore and extremely agonising to walk on. Lose 1 BRUTALITY and 2 VITALITY points. Retreating promptly before the acid can do any more damage, you then notice the acid is spreading! It then forms into a large, gigantic puddle which is too widespread for you to continue along this way. The figure who created this mess has long disappeared into the distance, so reluctantly you make the long walk back to the junction and plan an alternative route.
If you try west along Commerce Road, turn to **58**
Or to go north via Linzberg Staples, turn to **76**

91
Leaving the gambling halls, you may now visit either of the following places if you haven't already been to them:
The fighting arena. Turn to **42**
The tavern. Turn to **70**
If you're ready to continue with your adventure, turn to **84**

92
As soon as he realises that you are trying to escape, the man shoots a bullet from his pistol that hits the back of your head in no time at all. Slumping to the ground, you certainly won't be getting back up again. It is never a wise idea to underestimate one of Belveslade's most skilled and trained hunters. Your adventure ends here.

93

You approach Donowen to engage in further conversation but they're reluctant, instead mulling on what's happened.

"I hope you enjoy your prize money. Seek out the trader if you must, and try not to waste it in the tavern!" says Donowen as their wound is getting treated. Nodding in thanks, you turn around to meet the referee who hands back the five gold pieces you previously wagered plus an additional ten gold pieces for your victory (make the necessary amendments on your Adventure Sheet). With the feeling that now seems like a good opportunity to move on, you make tracks to see what else awaits within Belveslade.
Turn to **80**

94

He's got you stumped. As you desperately fumble around for something that will confirm what you've said is correct, the one who you suspect to be the Reaper Man releases a poisoned dart concealed in a hidden compartment within his armchair. It hits you straight in the chest almost instantaneously after being fired, and getting its full dosage causes you to lose consciousness whilst dropping to the floor. Before passing out, you hear footsteps approach you with the sound of a meat cleaver being gradually sharpened… destined to become his next luckless victim. Your adventure ends here.

95

Viamultain Avenue is host to many appetising food markets and stalls, reputable for the extraordinary range of fine delicacies it has to offer. Any chance of you stocking up on provisions however look remote given that the markets have now shut to cease trading until morning. There would have normally been a few cafeterias and restaurants attracting clientele, but these have now closed earlier than they would in the recent wake of the Reaper Man's activity. Unexpectedly though, you then happen to come across a butcher's which is seemingly open. Given everywhere else is locked and bolted, is it actually doing any business at this unusual time of night?

If you decide to explore the butcher's, turn to **34**
If you choose to continue past instead, turn to **71**

96

The combat champion is too strong for you and having no other choice but to admit defeat, you raise your hand to stop the fight. As soon as he notices this signal, the referee promptly steps back into the ring to intervene and bring the contest to an abrupt halt. He declares the champion as the winner and then sternly instructs you to leave the ring, which you do to a series of deafening boos and jeers from the crowd as you make your way out.

Turn to **80**

97

You are soon well clear of the venue and then come to another junction. Looking towards the west and the east, they both appear to trail off back to the south some few yards along their respective paths. Therefore, you conclude that the only sensible decision is to carry on northwards. After briefly glancing up for a moment, you find that you are now at Dervish Way.

Turn to **10**

98

Having exited the tavern, you may now wish to have a look inside either of the following locations if you haven't already done so:

The fighting arena. Turn to **42**
The gambling halls. Turn to **56**

If you'd rather continue with your adventure, turn to **84**

99

Reluctantly you tell Barr that you do not know of any other information which could help either of you track down the Reaper Man.

"Ah, how unfortunate!" is his response. "Well, I better not hold you up any more since we both have the same objective. You're free to go now – hope you locate him before I do!" He opens the door and then allows you to step back outside. You proceed towards the other end of the vennel to see where it leads. Twisting and turning for some distance, it then splits off into two. Whilst you're wondering which direction to follow, an unseen enemy suddenly stabs you in the back. As you fall to the ground, you cannot prevent yourself from then being stabbed once again. Unknown to you, the Reaper Man caught you leaving the hideout and then followed your movements through this alley. He has now made you his next victim as he sets about in finishing off the task whilst you lay defenceless. Your adventure ends here.

100

The Reaper Man screams again, but this time it is a wail of defeat. Kneeling on the floor, there is nothing he can do as you waste no time in plunging your sword into his heart. Ensuring your sword remains there until it is certain he has stopped breathing, eventually the ripper gasps his very last. You finally withdraw your sword and his lifeless body drops to the ground. Immediately afterwards, you hear the sound of two pairs of footsteps marching into the house. They belong to Barr and the Marquis, who look into the living room to see you standing over the Reaper Man's corpse.

"At last, Walkirsch is no more", says Barr. "The shadow of horror inflicted by his looming presence will no longer terrorise Belveslade's cobbled streets. You are to be highly commended, victorious warrior."

"Indeed", adds the Marquis. "This house is to be searched thoroughly at the earliest available opportunity. In the meantime, we will get you somewhere to rest before the moment you are well rewarded."

Later in the early hours of the morning, a bed is found and you sleep comfortably for quite a while. The residents of Belveslade will also be able to sleep peacefully for ages to come now that thanks to your efforts, the Reaper Man will no longer be hiding within their neighbourhood.

ULTRAVIOLATOR UNDERWORLD

ULTRAVIOLATOR UNDERWORLD

Introduction

Deep inside the Ordno Mines, a network of caves set beneath a rough stony mountain lurks a horrific tyrant known by the name of Gardav – who delights in nothing more than oppressing the well-meaning folk that live in the nearby village of Mottinghurst.

Executing his actions with the aid of a gruesome creature known only as the Krudorff, Gardav will order this monster to seek out and capture any unfortunate individuals wandering aimlessly in or near the village.

People in Mottinghurst have had enough of Gardav's deplorable means of persecution, but most especially one gentleman who happens to be the only person to have successfully thwarted the Krudorff's attacks.

Echoing the desire of his fellow villagers in putting an end to Gardav's reign of terror, the survivor Alton Sagar has been actively looking for a warrior bold enough to enter the Ordno Mines and stop this twisted ruler more commonly recognised as "the Ultraviolator".

Chance has it that one day you're visiting Mottinghurst, having been made aware of the Ultraviolator's cruel antics. When the villagers learn that you are in the vicinity, they look for Alton Sagar to inform him that a warrior is around who could finally overturn their years of misery.

He is a slightly old but hardened fellow, and upon hearing this news Alton Sagar wastes no time in putting on hold what he's currently doing to meet you next by the village's granite monument.

Excited when he catches sight of your presence, Alton Sagar then gives you a warm greeting before giving a full introduction.

"My friend, no doubt you will have heard the many stories of our plight under Gardav!" he explains. "I trust that you can help us get of rid of this scourge. If so, then you will be handsomely rewarded for eliminating the Ultraviolator as well as his pet monster. As well as a payment of gold, you will also gain recognition which I personally believe to be of a far greater value. Where previous explorers and spelunkers have attempted to overcome him but failed, I'm confident that at last we have someone who can successfully triumph."

"Ok then", you nod. "I've heard all these tales of the unwanted suffering that Gardav has inflicted upon your people and I accept your mission."

Despair becomes encouragement as Alton Sagar and the other villagers smile upon hearing you take up this challenge. They tell you that the Ordno Mines are located to the north of Mottinghurst, as well as show you a map detailing the best route to get there. As an advance gesture of thanks, you are provided with three portions of food to eat during your adventure.

Eventually the time comes for you to set off towards the Ordno Mines and many of Mottinghurst's villagers wish you luck. Following the route suggested, you come to the mountain that hosts the mines several hours later. After a short rest you begin to look for the entrance that will lead into the depths of the mines and when you do find it, you take a deep breath before taking a peek inside to get a feel of what Gardav might have lying in wait for you…

Now turn to **1**

1
Cautiously you begin to navigate the deep sloping path that leads on from the entrance of the mines. With careful footing, you eventually reach the surface of the bottom then start to plan how you'll negotiate the various passages that will lead on to Gardav's lair.
Once you've begun to make just a few paces afterwards however, you come across the body of a spiky haired man lying on the ground! Recoiling for a slight moment, you then compose yourself to look at the body; the man does not appear to breathe and Gardav may have situated him here as a warning to anyone foolish enough to think it's going to be easy infiltrating the domain within.
If you decide to investigate the body, turn to **55**
If you'd rather leave it where it is, turn to **66**

2
You reach the bank of a fast-flowing stream of water. Glancing across, there are a number of large stepping stones leading from the bank you're presently standing on to another bank situated on the other side. The ceiling above this stretch of water is quite low and has some metallic rungs fixed into some of the shorter stalactites located above the stepping stones. Using the stones in some form appears to be the only way of crossing in order to reach the further parts of the mines.
If you have a rope and grappling hook, turn to **15**
If you have a plank of wood, turn to **27**
Otherwise, turn to **39**

3
The meats are very delicious and have also been garnished with some nourishingly tasty herbs. Restore your VITALITY to its starting score. Now, will you:
Try on the armour? Turn to **40**
Or leave the room? Turn to **98**

4

You are so occupied with continuing down the lowering tunnel that you're completely taken by surprise when an area of weakened floor crumbles beneath your feet. It reveals a deep pit underneath and without anything to grip on to, you fall down then land on a sharp bed of spikes which instantly impale you upon impact. Your adventure ends here.

5

The plank of wood you pick up is at least a couple of metres in length and you get the feeling that it could be of some use further down the mines. Just as you are about to carry on though, you glimpse something gleaming amongst the remaining planks and are curious as to whether this could also be of interest.
If you would like to take a closer look, turn to **42**
Or to continue on your way, turn to **71**

6

You grab the crystal out of your backpack and hold it up before you. Immediately the crystal's colourful rays glow as they overpower and absorb the flickering light of the tunnel. All around where you stand becomes filled with a dazzling assortment of blinding colour; then looking at the shadow you notice it has dropped its weapon and is cowering miserably as it becomes soaked up by the resulting brightness. A short while later and it has dissipated into nothing, followed by the light emitted from the crystal gradually dimming. There is no trace of the shadow ever having been present within the mines and soon the only light source emitted from the object you're holding are the rays within the very crystal itself. Happily returning it to your backpack, you then continue onwards to find out what may possibly await you next.
Turn to **50**

7

After some time pacing along the tunnel you're currently walking down, the clanking sound of armour is then heard moving towards you. Drawing your sword in case the worst happens, your fears are confirmed when a giant figure clad head to toe in metal appears and unsheathes their own weapon at the sight of your presence. This is Ornitram, one of Gardav's main guards. Without the need for any meaningful words, he simply growls ferociously and begins to advance with his own sword raised. Knowing that there is no option but to do battle with him, will you:

Throw a vial of liquid at Ornitram?　　　　Turn to **21**
Hurl a smoke ball instead?　　　　　　　　Turn to **35**
Get ready to fight with your own sword?　　Turn to **64**

8

You are able to jump a long distance which gets you to safety when Gardav's improvisational bomb explodes upon hitting the surface. When the bomb does explode, you are crouching down and covering your ears from the deafening explosion. After a few moments later, the ferocious blast has subsided. Picking yourself slowly off the floor once you know it's safe to do so, you then take the opportunity to look across the debris-strewn cavern. There you eventually see your adversary lying motionless and face down on the ground. He does not get up, nor will he do so again.
Turn to **41**

9

Taking a closer inspection at the wall, it does have some rough edges that can be used as makeshift holders for your hands and feet. You proceed to use these in order to climb upwards. Roll two dice.
If it's less than or equal to your PHYSICALITY, turn to **36**
If the total is greater than your PHYSICALITY, turn to **82**

10

A few metres on, you notice a door set inside the left wall of the tunnel. Walking up to have a closer look, the door has an iron grille for a window. Could there be anything interesting lurking beyond?
If you go up to the door and investigate further, turn to **29**
If you leave things be and ignore it, turn to **43**

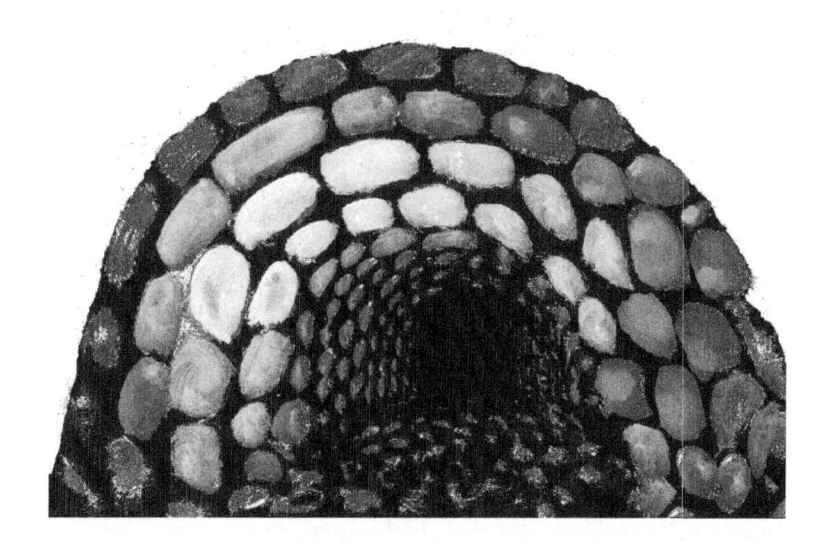

11

You carefully remove the backpack from the skeleton in case anything untoward happens. To your amazement, the skeleton does not move whilst you're examining the backpack's contents. Inside the main compartment are a rope and grappling hook; you decide it would be worth taking these with you (add them to your Adventure Sheet). Once you've happily transferred them to your own backpack, you take another look at the skeleton which keeps firmly rooted to its spot. Wondering what led to its demise, you then continue on your way.
Turn to **2**

12

Making the decision to go left, you head down the tunnel leading off from that direction. A short while later, it twists round with a well full of liquid forming the central part of the corner. The paths around the well both reconvene into a single path on the other side which will take you onwards from its bend.
If you walk around the left-hand side of the well, turn to **19**
If you walk around the right-hand side of the well, turn to **32**
Or to test the liquid that's inside the well itself, turn to **67**

13

This tunnel eventually descends into darkness as its lowering ceiling forces you to crawl along on your hands and knees, uncertain as for how long it continues on for.
If you keep on crawling through relentlessly, turn to **52**
If you return to the safety of the passageway, turn to **87**

14

Not trusting the appearance of this woman, you proceed forwards with your sword at the ready. She responds by reaching into a pocket inside her jacket and pulling out a black coloured powder which she then blows into your face. Instantly you lose consciousness and slump on to the floor…
Awakening after some period of time, you compose yourself to find that you're back at the intersection. Looking around, the woman is nowhere to be seen – and neither are your food parcels or any collected items which she has stolen! Cross all these off your Adventure Sheet. The only possessions still remaining are your sword and backpack. Frustrated, you curse the woman but decide not to return down the tunnel in fear of her catching you again to inflict an even worse punishment. Instead having a moment to contemplate where the other two tunnels might lead, do you choose to take:
The left-hand tunnel. Turn to **31**
Or the central tunnel. Turn to **62**

15

The rope you have is thin enough to fit through the metal rungs attached to the stalactites, so you pull it out of your backpack and thread it through the first rung in order to swing from the bank on to the first stepping stone. You accomplish this without any problems, and remove the rope from its existing rung to thread it through the next one attached to the adjacent stalactite. Swinging again on to the next stepping stone, you repeat the process until you safely land on the opposite bank of this stretch of water. As soon as you get there, you unthread the rope from the last rung and return it to your backpack.
Turn to **91**

16

The colourful rays of the crystal shine around you and fill the cavern.
"How pretty!" mocks Gardav. "You must have obtained that from the spectral remains of the necromancer who was foolish enough to betray me. And like him, you'll now find out it's uselessness against my power…"
Without wanting to waste any more time, Gardav leaps towards you before landing an incredible blow from his fist that knocks the crystal out of your hand and also sends you reeling into the nearest cavern wall. The strength and unpredictability of Gardav's fist results in you losing 4 VITALITY points. If you're still alive, you get back up and prepare to fight as your adversary charges to finish you off.
Turn to **79**

17

You decide to keep going straight on and soon come to an area where it turns to the left. In the corner lies a bundle of long wooden planks.
If you would like to take a plank of wood, turn to **5**
If not, turn to **48**

18

Holding up the crystal, you hope for the Krudorff to be mesmerised by its rays. The beast advances towards where you stand but once it's near, claws the crystal out of your hands with a powerful strike where the item then smashes into pieces upon making contact with a surface. Remove the crystal from your Adventure Sheet. Whilst in disbelief, you're unprepared for the Krudorff's second blow that produces a deep gash on your chest; deduct 4 VITALITY points. If you are still alive, there is now no other option but to fight this creature.
Turn to **97**

19

Walking around the left-hand side of the well, you come to the decision that it's perhaps best not to check the potentially odd liquid inside it. Nothing of incident happens, and after a few minutes you are of considerable distance away from the well and continuing your journey through this tunnel as it veers northwards.
Turn to **50**

20

The critters you encountered were Gardav's own pets with many of them exposed to a toxic substance. In turn, this made them go rabid and having been bitten by them could have harmful consequences for you. Roll one die to find out.

If you roll:
1 or 2 -   No effect.
3 or 4 -   Lose 1 BRUTALITY point.
5 or 6 -   Lose 1 BRUTALITY, 1 PHYSICALITY, 1 MENTALITY and reduce your VITALITY by half (rounding any fractions down).

Now turn to **49**

21

The vial immediately smashes upon contact with Ornitram's armour. He snarls in pain as the vial, which is in fact a potion of rust, eats into his metal breastplates for a few moments. Now that you have used it, cross this item off your Adventure Sheet. You've weakened Ornitram but he reacts by rushing towards you with rage, determined to have his revenge:

ORNITRAM
BRUTALITY 6 VITALITY 10

If you win, turn to **77**

22

You manage to dodge the man's attack, but now he stands up and lunges in your direction with an uncontrollable frenzy! Drawing your sword, you prepare to defend yourself:

INSANE MAN
BRUTALITY 6 VITALITY 6

If you win, turn to **44**

23

Flandetch smiles when you tell him the correct answer.

"So, you paid attention to my etchings on the wall from my attempted escape!" he laughs. "Unfortunately, Ornitram found and captured me before I could reach the safety of outside. My companion Wilderal was also captured in our failed attempt to despatch Gardav, but because he went insane Wilderal was allowed to roam the tunnels freely as Gardav knew he would attack anyone he laid eyes upon. Wilderal always had a vial of yellow-coloured liquid in his possession which believe it or not, is in fact a potion of rust. Not sure if you are to or have encountered him, but either way if you were to get hold of this vial it would be very useful in your mission."

You thank Flandetch for this information. There is nothing else you can do for him at this present time, but you promise to ensure his freedom should you manage to defeat Gardav. Bidding each other farewell, your attention then returns to continuing down this particular stretch of tunnel you're currently exploring.

Turn to **96**

24

Uncorking the potion, you throw its contents towards the Krudorff. Some of the liquid makes contact with the beast, causing it to roar angrily as if it had just been hit with acid. Cross the potion off your Adventure Sheet. Whilst it has indeed been effective and caused some damage, you get ready to finish off the monstrous Krudorff with your sword as it responds by charging angrily in the direction where you're standing:

KRUDORFF
BRUTALITY 8 VITALITY 6

If you win, turn to **81**

25

You smile, greeting the woman courteously.
"And what can I help you with?" she replies with a stern expression, somewhat unimpressed with your approach. How do you respond?
Tell her that you're here to defeat Gardav.   Turn to **47**
State that you're trying to escape the mines. Turn to **63**

26

Crawling down the tunnel for some distance, everything around you soon becomes pitch black further along. It is unknown how much longer this tunnel stretches on for.
If you keep going, turn to **4**
If you retreat to the safety of the corridor, turn to **59**

27

The plank is long enough to span across two stepping stones, so you make sure it is safely on top of them before using the plank to get across the stones. You're nearly at the other side of the bank when all of a sudden you unexpectedly kick the plank after landing on a stone and watch helplessly as it rolls off the stones where it was evenly balanced, then splashes into the water before getting swept away downstream. You now have no option but to jump across the last few stepping stones. Although the stones aren't far apart from each other, the ordeal of crossing the river is starting to become tiring. Roll two dice.
If it's less than or equal to your MENTALITY, turn to **68**
If the total is greater than your MENTALITY, turn to **99**

28

You open the bottle and hurl the potion's contents at Gardav. It appears to have no effect on him, when suddenly your opponent erupts into peals of laughter.
"What is dangerous to metal has the opposite reaction to my strength!" he taunts. "I don't need a puny weapon to destroy you, so allow my fists to execute the talking…"
To your horror, you realise the potion has made Gardav more powerful! Almost upon you and getting ready to pound your flesh, you must face what is now a harder final encounter:

GARDAV
BRUTALITY 9 VITALITY 20

If you somehow reduce his VITALITY to 2 points or less, turn to **58**

29

Walking up to the door, you peer through the grille to find out what might lurk beyond.
"Leave me alone!" a voice shouts from the cell inside. You try pushing the door open to see who is there, but it's locked shut and no amount of strength will be able to force it open.
"Go away, I don't need any more unwanted distress!" adds the voice, clearly becoming agitated by your actions.
If you try talking to the voice, turn to **51**
If you do as the voice wishes, turn to **70**

30

Looking at the door more closely, you find an X-shaped lock set into it. Could you potentially have a particular item that will open up the lock? If so, then you know it has a letter embossed on one end and a number on the other; turn to the section which corresponds with this number. Otherwise, you regretfully abandon the wooden door and continue onwards. In which case, turn to **86**

31

This section initially appears uneventful, but once the tunnel curves to the right you come across some writing on the wall that appears to have been etched using chalk. You go and take a closer look at the writing. Roll two dice.
If it's less than or equal to your MENTALITY, turn to **46**
If the total is greater than your MENTALITY, turn to **85**

32

You walk around the well's right-hand side, unaware that it is in fact slightly leaking near its base. A very thin trickle of the well's liquid becomes soaked up by your boots and seeps into your feet. Only when you look down at the ground then hiss in pain do you realise that this liquid is in fact acid. Lose 2 VITALITY points. Hurriedly you begin to pick up pace and run as fast as you can to avoid sustaining any further damage from the leaking well.
Turn to **50**

33

The man's sharp fingernails claw into your face, leaving a red gash. Lose 2 VITALITY points. As you retreat a couple of steps backwards, the man stands up then lunges towards you in a fit of rage! Unsheathing your sword, you get ready to stop him inflicting any further attacks:

INSANE MAN
BRUTALITY 6 VITALITY 6

If you win, turn to **44**

34

Making the decision to head right, you proceed to make your way along this new stretch. The tunnel continues for some time before eventually veering round a corner, and looking ahead you notice an odd flickering light from another corner nearby. When you get to this new corner, there is a manifestation from the light which reveals itself to be a shadow armed with a sword who begins to swing its weapon towards you! Flinching back to avoid its blows, you respond by drawing your own sword in retaliation. Using it to lash out at the deadly shadow, it soon becomes apparent that what you're attempting to do is futile. The apparition is just standing there, clearly immune to the strikes from your sword. Then it occurs to you; how is it possible to wound something that does not appear to have a physical presence? Withdrawing momentarily so that an alternative course of action can be thought out here, you desperately look for a possible item that will help overcome this sinister assailant. Do you have any of the following:

A crystal.	Turn to **6**
A pouch of shroud mist.	Turn to **72**
A smoke ball.	Turn to **83**

If you have none of these items (or prefer not to use them), turn to **95**

35

Hurriedly grabbing the smoke ball from out of your backpack, you then hurl it towards Ornitram. But moments later you are staring in disbelief as it rebounds harmlessly off his armour before landing on the ground. Ornitram responds by picking up the smoke ball then crushing it to pieces with his gauntleted hand. You have foolishly wasted the smoke ball's power and now lost it permanently (cross it off your Adventure Sheet). Without any time to regret what's just occurred, you get ready to face Ornitram in battle.
Turn to **64**

36

You successfully climb over the top of the wall and jump off down to the other side, landing safely on the ground beneath. This is no cause to celebrate though when you find an array of deadly bugs, centipedes, spiders and worms surrounding the point where you stand! Not wanting to be overwhelmed by them, you reach for your sword to fend off these vermin. Fight the insects as if they were a single creature:

CAVERNOUS CRITTERS
BRUTALITY 7 VITALITY 8

If you win, turn to **57**

37

Emptying out the shroud mist into the palm of your hand, you blow it towards Gardav's direction. The nearby fire is extinguished, followed by the cavern falling into complete darkness. Only then does Gardav utter a response.
"Do you think I can be impeded by these blackened surroundings?" comes the inquisitive tone. "Too bad I'm still able to sense the unwelcome odour of your reeking flesh…"
Next to no time, your neck is seized by a powerful hand. Such is the strength of Gardav's grip, he proceeds to strangle what life remains out of you until you're asphyxiated completely. Chuckling to himself, the despicable tyrant then drops your exanimate body on to the floor knowing that you won't be getting back up. Your adventure ends here.

38

Remaining silent, the woman doesn't say anything as you walk past her. A moment afterwards, some curiosity develops inside you and thoughts occur as to if she has given chase. Turning your head round, she in fact appears to have disappeared out of sight. You shrug and carry on your way.
Turn to **80**

39

There is no option but to jump across each stepping stone in order to get to the bank on the other side. Negotiating the first set of stones without any difficulty, you then notice the next stone that needs to be jumped on spans a wider gap compared to the previous stepping stones. As the distance to jump is larger than what you've performed so far, some expert leaping will be needed here if you are to continue ahead. Roll two dice.
If it's less than or equal to your PHYSICALITY, turn to **56**
If the total is greater than your PHYSICALITY, turn to **73**

40

You find that the armour fits you perfectly. It will no doubt be of useful aid during combats that may be encountered in the stages leading up to Gardav. Add 1 BRUTALITY point (even if this results in going above your starting score). Delighted at feeling better equipped thanks to this acquisition, you decide on what to do next.
Eat the meats? Turn to **3**
Or leave the room? Turn to **98**

41

At last, Gardav is dead and will no longer bring a foreboding sense of despair to the innocent people of Mottinghurst. Having infiltrated his lair and putting an end to the despot's nefarious ways, you search the cavern to find if there's anything useful. Only a decent length of rope is found after a thorough search, and if you're not already in possession of any rope then you can take this with you. At the very least it will safely get you back across the river.
Turn to **100**

42

You put your hand in amongst the remaining planks to investigate the gleaming object. Within seconds you feel yourself being grasped by something which causes you to panic and make your focus hazy; lose 1 MENTALITY point. Scrambling to remove planks with your other hand so you can discover what's firmly holding you, this reveals itself to be a spectral hand which is beginning to slowly drain you of any power you currently possess! Using your free hand to get hold of your sword, you pull it out as fast as you can in an attempt to avoid it depleting even more of your energy. As soon as it's been fully unsheathed, you start to hack away at this apparition before it can inflict any additional damage. Due to the present cumbersome position you're in, you must reduce your BRUTALITY by 1 for the duration of this combat only. In addition, the spectral hand drains your VITALITY by 1 point each attack round, regardless if your Attack Rating is higher during that particular round. If you lose an attack round, you therefore suffer the loss of 3 VITALITY points in total so it's important to secure victory extremely quickly!

SPECTRAL HAND
BRUTALITY 8 VITALITY 10

If you win, turn to **60**

43

Not deeming there to be anything worth examining through the door, you continue to walk down the tunnel. There certainly must be something else along the way which can be of somewhat more significant interest, you think to yourself as this present trek carries on for some distance further ahead.
Turn to **96**

44

The man slumps to the ground. You wait for a moment in case he bursts into life again, but this time he is truly dead. Once it becomes obvious to yourself that he will no longer attack, you check over his garments in case he happens to hold anything that might be useful. After a thorough inspection, you manage to find inside one pocket a vial of yellow-coloured liquid. Decide whether to take this with you before setting off through the passage.
Turn to **90**

45

Upon having a look, you conclude that the door isn't going to be leading anywhere useful. Therefore, you choose not to bother with it and instead continue onwards.
Turn to **86**

46

Inspecting the writing, a lot of it appears to be of randomised gibberish. Despite that, something does at least catch your eye which you're able to make out as described below:

F. 𝍷𝍷𝍷𝍷𝍷 𝍷𝍷𝍷𝍷𝍷 𝍷𝍷𝍷𝍷𝍷 𝍷𝍷𝍷𝍷𝍷 𝍷𝍷𝍷

On the assumption that it could be noteworthy, you make a note of this information before proceeding down the tunnel.
Turn to **10**

47

You inform the woman of your mission, and appearing pleased on hearing what you've been assigned to do she relaxes with a faint smile.

"I am glad that someone is here to rid these infernal mines of Gardav!" she replies. "Whilst I have no intention of venturing into the outside world, his presence here makes my habitat within this domain somewhat uncomfortable. Though I dare not attempt to overcome him or his servants, thankfully he acknowledges the capability of my powers and decides to leave me alone. My name is Vilquin, and it's a pleasure to meet you. Be assured I do have something that will help along the way…"

Reaching inside her jacket pocket, she then pulls out a black pouch before handing it over to you.

"This pouch contains shroud mist which can hinder some enemies you might encounter further within these mines. However, there is only enough for one use so I recommend you deploy it extremely carefully. Good luck!"

You thank Vilquin for this item and tuck it away safely (make a note of the shroud mist on your Adventure Sheet). Wishing her farewell, you turn round the corner to walk down a new stretch of tunnel.

Turn to **80**

48

Leaving the planks of wood in case something horrid lurks beneath, you follow a new turn in the path you're on and wonder where it leads.

Turn to **2**

49

You waste no time in darting towards the stretch of tunnel ahead of you before any more of these gruesome insects surface to attack.

Turn to **75**

50

Soon you arrive at yet another junction. There are two paths here for consideration, but after hearing a deep growl come from one of them you sense that your target is nearby. Intrigued, you decide to investigate this sound to find out if it's what you've been assigned to despatch.
Turn to **76**

51

Telling the voice that you mean no harm, you state your mission to defeat the evil ruler Gardav.

"Nice to know someone's intending to end his crimes!" says the voice more assuredly. "His accomplice Ornitram keeps me detained here for the master's pleasure. My name is Flandetch and I once tried to rid this land of Gardav, but I was unsuccessful and thrown into these wretched confines as punishment. You may know how many years I've been stuck here, and if you do then I can help out somehow."

Do you know the length of time Flandetch has been kept prisoner? Should that be the case, turn to the section which corresponds with that exact number of years. If you don't know or turn to a section which makes no sense, then you must instead turn to **84**

52

After a while the tunnel comes to an end. Feeling around, all you recognise is jagged rock. Then your hand touches a spherical-like object; you pick it up and work your way backwards to investigate what it is. Moments later, you have re-emerged in the passage. The object you are holding is a glass ball filled with whirring smoke, and looks as if it could be useful. Opening up your backpack, you place the smoke ball into it (you should also make a note of this item on your Adventure Sheet). Then you decide on what to do next.

If you try out the right-hand tunnel, turn to **26**
Otherwise, you continue onwards. Turn to **78**

53

Pouring the contents of the shroud mist into the palm of your hand, there's no time to lose. You then blow it towards the direction of the advancing Krudorff, just as it's within an inch of reaching you. The mist covers the beast entirely which causes it to step back for a moment, unable to shake off the effect of what you've used against it. In fact, the shroud mist has completely blinded the Krudorff! This gives you the opportunity to pull out your sword and thrust it into the creature's heart where the blade will gradually put an end to its existence.
Turn to **81**

54

The tunnel you are walking down twists for a while before arriving at another intersection. Noticing something down one of the other tunnels, you make your way towards it.
Turn to **75**

55

As you approach the man, you hear what sounds like breathing so maybe he's not dead after all. You're on the verge of kneeling down beside him when he suddenly turns over and attempts to lash out with his hand! Desperately in a panic, you try to flinch back. Roll two dice.
If it's less than or equal to your PHYSICALITY, turn to **22**
If the total is greater than your PHYSICALITY, turn to **33**

56

You make it on to the stepping stone and look ahead to see the other side of the bank looming closer. There are only a few more stones to get across but the toll of repeatedly jumping from stone to stone is beginning to wear you down. Roll two dice.
If it's less than or equal to your MENTALITY, turn to **68**
If the total is greater than your MENTALITY, turn to **99**

57
Did you get wounded during this battle?
If so, turn to **20**
If not, turn to **49**

58
Your opponent staggers back, aware that he is on the brink of defeat. Retreating to the back of the cavern, Gardav reaches down to pick up a round item wrapped up in a white cloth before returning to the burning drum can where he ignites the item he is holding.
"I'm not done yet!" rages Gardav as he launches the enkindled projectile towards where you are standing. Instinctively, you try to leap out of the way. Roll two dice.
If it's less than or equal to your PHYSICALITY, turn to **8**
If the total is greater than your PHYSICALITY, turn to **89**

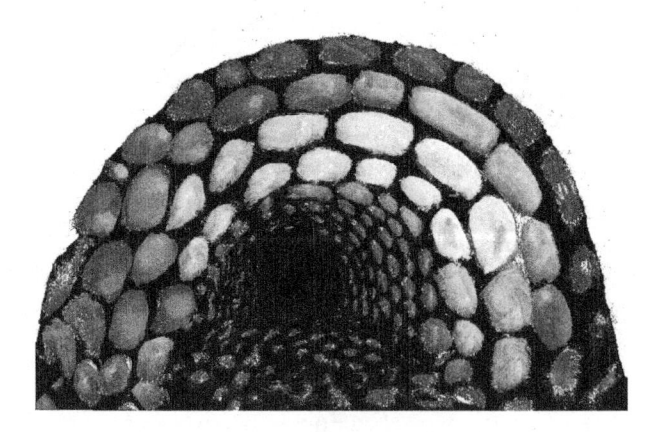

59
Thinking it best to retrace your steps and make your way backwards, you decide not to chance it in this particular tunnel. Eventually light shines from behind and you are back out, standing up to find yourself in the passage one again.
To try the left-hand tunnel, turn to **13**
Or to continue onwards, turn to **78**

60

Exhausted from the battle, you lean by the wall to regain your breath. Keeping a close eye on the spectral hand it case it twitches once again, you are relieved when after a short period of time it doesn't move at all. You walk back over to the planks in order to investigate what the apparition was holding with its other hand. After removing some of the long wooden planks, you look down and discover the item to be a crystal of many shimmering rays. Carefully extracting it out of the hand's grip, you then place it into your backpack in case it should become useful later. Next you pick up the first plank of wood you initially chose and also take this with you (make a note of both the crystal and the plank of wood on your Adventure Sheet). Following the path to the left, you decide it best not to find out what ghastly being can lay claim to the spectral hands.
Turn to **2**

61

Hurling the smoke ball at the Krudorff, you have underestimated the beast's agility as it dodges your attack whilst the ball smashes harmlessly into the wall opposite. You've wasted the smoke ball and have now lost it (cross this item off your Adventure Sheet). With the dreaded creature beginning to advance towards you, the only possibility remaining is to get ready and fight.
Turn to **97**

62

You opt to keep going straight ahead but this soon appears to be a foolish decision when you then come to a brick wall that is about four metres in height which blocks your progress. The wall does not reach the ceiling though; it may be possible to climb over it in order to continue.
If you would like to try this, turn to **9**
If you retreat back to the intersection, turn to **74**

63

"Lost, are you?" scoffs the woman. "To get stuck in this network of tunnels can only serve as a warning to retrace your steps and find the way back out yourself. Now begone!" Sighing, you turn round the corner knowing that you won't be getting any further help from her. A new stretch of tunnel lies ahead and following it, you hope that it will lead to somewhere useful.
Turn to **80**

64

Ornitram is a skilled warrior, but you're confident in defeating him. With your sword at the ready, you prepare to clash against this guardian in a fight to the death:

ORNITRAM
BRUTALITY 8 VITALITY 12

If you win, turn to **77**

65

You grab the smoke ball from your backpack. As soon as he notices it, Gardav's fearless stance turns to one of anxiety.
"Now, why would you want to use that?" he asks. Sensing that he is alarmed by the presence of the smoke ball, you don't hesitate in smashing it on to the hard ground in order to release the smoke. Upon shattering, the smoke escapes to fill the entire cavern. Very briefly do you see Gardav raising his arms before the smoke becomes so thick that you are then unable to see anything whatsoever. This goes on until the smoke begins to evaporate. Finally, it clears and you look towards the direction of Gardav. It appears that the smoke acted like toxic fumes upon making contact with his body, having completely stripped away his flesh and leaving nothing of him apart from a pitiful skeleton.
Turn to **41**

66
Deciding not to check over the man, you continue onwards.
Turn to **90**

67
You put your hand into the well and instantly scream loudly in painful agony. It turns out to be severely corrosive acid! Lose 1 BRUTALITY, 1 MENTALITY, 1 PHYSICALITY and one die roll's worth of VITALITY points. If you are still alive, you hurriedly raise your hand back out and get away as far as you can from the cursed well. After a while, you stop to bandage your wounded hand so that it's best protected as can possibly be whilst ruefully contemplating that stupid decision you've made. Then you stagger along into the tunnel ahead.
Turn to **50**

68
Pulling yourself together, you summon what remaining energy there is inside of you and safely make it across the last few of the stepping stones. Whilst it may not have been easy during particular moments, at least you're now standing on the opposite bank having safely negotiated the fast-flowing water's stream.
Turn to **91**

69
Taking the rod out of your backpack, you then go and place its X-shaped end into the lock. After working out which way you should twist the rod, the door then opens and you find yourself inside Ornitram's quarters. Various trinkets he managed to confiscate from previous victims are scattered on plinths within the confines of the room, but the most appealing items here are a selection of meats on a table plus a torso-sized armour hanging on a wall that could ably protect your chest. What would you like to do?

Eat the meats.	Turn to **3**
Try on the armour.	Turn to **40**

70
Whoever resides within the cell obviously does not want to be agitated. Leaving them be as requested, you walk away to continue your journey.
Turn to **96**

71
You decide not to take a chance in removing the item glistening within the bundle of planks and instead proceed to make your way straight down the new turn in the tunnel, carrying the singular plank of wood you reckon might be useful later (add it to your Adventure Sheet if you haven't already done so).
Turn to **2**

72

You take out the pouch and pour out the shroud mist on to your hand before blowing it in the direction of the shadow. The flickering light is extinguished and all of the area surrounding you becomes pitch dark. However, shadows thrive in dark environments and the next thing you know is that you're being relentlessly struck blow after repeated blow by a sword whose blade feels similar to that you caught sight of being held by the shadow. Unable to defend yourself properly by not knowing your adversary's precise location, it is not long until you are fatally cut down. As you slump to the ground in defeat, eventually you are finished off by the shadow's razor-sharp weapon. Your adventure ends here.

73

Falling short of the distance required to land on the stepping stone, instead you plunge into the stream of running water and are swept to an unpleasant fate awaiting you nearby. Your adventure ends here.

74

The wall appears too high for you to climb, so you return to the intersection and decide which of the other paths would be a better option to take.
To go down the left-hand tunnel, turn to **31**
To go down the right-hand tunnel, turn to **93**

75

Making your way along, you come across a motionless skeleton resting up against a wall. It's sat on the ground and holding a backpack that's similar to yours, but nothing else of interest.
If you investigate the skeleton's backpack, turn to **11**
Or if you prefer to leave it in case a deadly trap is sprung, turn to **88**

76

You tread carefully through the foreboding tunnel, which has dashes of blood splattered across its walls. This gruesome corridor eventually opens out into a wider cavern, and accompanying the gore-daubed streaks are the bony remains of previous hapless victims. A solitary exit is located on the other side of the cavern, and it is from beyond here what first gave a deep growl bellows again upon sensing your presence. But this time, the sound it gives out is a feral and savage roar...

Then the creature makes its way out of the opening located directly opposite where you stand, and only when it unfurls itself to full height do you realise it is indeed the very one that has been terrorising the people of Mottinghurst. The Krudorff is three metres tall with its body mostly comprising of taut coriaceous skin. It also has horns protruding from either side of its head, and its fingers and toes all end in razor sharp talons. Upon sighting you, this hideous beast lets out another mighty ear-deafening sound. Looking directly at its hate-filled eyes, you acknowledge the urgency within yourself to take immediate action before this monster lurches forward to attack. What will you use?

A crystal.	Turn to **18**
A potion of rust.	Turn to **24**
A pouch of shroud mist.	Turn to **53**
A smoke ball.	Turn to **61**

If you have none of these items (or prefer not to use them), turn to **97**

77

At last, Ornitram falls. Rummaging in his pockets, you find a small bottle of matured brandy which you take a swig from. The contents instantly revitalise you; gain 4 VITALITY points. Inside another pocket you find a rod that has a X embossed on one end and the number 69 on its opposite end. This could be potentially useful later on so you drop it inside your backpack (make a note of the rod on your Adventure Sheet). Continuing onwards, you relish the fact that Ornitram is no longer going to be a threat within these mines. Turn to **2**

78

You soon come to an intersection which splits off into three different tunnels. Peering down each tunnel, none of them have any indication they are the correct route for you to follow. Therefore, you'll need to decide for yourself as to which of these tunnels is the best way to progress:

The left-hand tunnel.	Turn to **31**
The central tunnel.	Turn to **62**
The right-hand tunnel.	Turn to **93**

79

Gardav advances towards you with his fists raised. Whilst doing so he flashes a broad, wide grin across his face. This antagonist is most definitely unafraid of the paltry trouble someone like you could possibly have against him.

"No weapon can match the power of these!" he boasts. You respond by drawing your sword in an attempt to prove that he's undeniably wrong. The ultimate battle then commences:

GARDAV
BRUTALITY 9 VITALITY 10

If you reduce Gardav's VITALITY to 2 points or any less, turn to **58**

80

Arriving at a junction, there is one path that leads directly ahead and the other branching off to the left. Which route will you choose?
To continue going ahead, turn to **17**
To take the left-hand path, turn to **94**

81

The Krudorff lies motionless on the ground before you. Wiping its repulsive blood off from the blade of your sword, you then hear a spine-chilling laugh echoing loudly from the exit opposite.
"Didn't expect anyone to kill my powerful servant!" chuckles the sinister voice which can only be that of Gardav. "Not that it really matters, for I know of outer realms where I can easily get hold of another horrific behemoth that can frighten and seize those hapless souls of Mottinghurst. Unless that is of course, you intend to take me on personally in a fight to the death. Be warned however; the capabilities I possess are of a substantially different nature to what you've just vanquished. Looking forward to duelling with you, for I happen to reside in the next chamber…"
Without needing any further incentive, you take a few moments to get yourself ready before proceeding through the exit so that you can silence this depraved gloating adversary once and for all.
Turn to **92**

82

You are almost at the top when you suddenly lose your grip on the wall, causing you to fall down and land somewhat painfully. Lose 1 BRUTALITY and 2 VITALITY points. If you are still alive, slowly you pick yourself off the ground in agony before concluding that it's best not to attempt climbing the wall again.
Turn to **74**

83

Launching the smoke ball towards the shadow, you then watch in disbelief as the ball vanishes to no effect. It has in fact been absorbed by the shadow and now you have lost the smoke ball permanently (cross it off your Adventure Sheet). Desperately, you look for something else that might be able to get you past this situation:
To use a crystal, turn to **6**
To try a pouch of shroud mist, turn to **72**
Or if you have neither of these, turn to **95**

84

Flandetch says that he is unable to help you. Shrugging your shoulders with a sigh, you reluctantly continue on your way.
Turn to **96**

85

Try as you might, you cannot work out the meaning of the writing. Disappointed, there is nothing else but to carry on walking down the tunnel in a state of befuddlement.
Turn to **10**

86

You come to another junction with paths leading off the left and right. Both paths happen to look as similar and uninviting as the other.
To head left, turn to **12**
Or to go right, turn to **34**

87

The darkness of the tunnel becomes too intimidating and so you begin crawling backwards to the safety of the passage. Soon light emerges and moments later you find yourself back in familiar surroundings.
If you would like to try the right-hand tunnel, turn to **26**
If you prefer to continue onwards instead, turn to **78**

88

Staying away from the skeleton, you are concerned that it will come to life if you touch it. Hastily, you then stride a fast pace to avoid the skeleton as you continue onwards.
Turn to **2**

89

A dazzling array of white flares shoot out widespread from the explosive device upon making impact with a wall, and you are not far enough to avoid being hit by its searing blast. Lose 4 VITALITY points. If you're still alive, you extinguish any flames from your clothing before looking towards Gardav as he lies unresponsive on the floor.
Turn to **41**

90

You arrive at an area with two tunnels set into the walls, directly facing one another. Examining them reveals nothing but apparent endless darkness leading beyond them both.
If you explore the tunnel in the left-hand wall, turn to **13**
If you see what the right-hand tunnel contains, turn to **26**
If you ignore both tunnels and continue onwards, turn to **78**

91

After resting for a moment, you pick yourself up and proceed to stride down the tunnel which leads off from the bank. Eventually you reach a wooden door on the left that has no windows or even a handle to push or pull the door open.
To investigate the door further, turn to **30**
Or to leave it behind, turn to **45**

92

Rushing through a brief section of tunnel, you then emerge into a rather expansive cavern that's much larger than the one you just encountered. Around you are relatively sparse and basic furnishings, with the area being lit by a fire burning inside a metal drum can. Standing in the middle of this cavern is none other than Gardav; a man roughly the same height as you but far more muscular in appearance and wearing ragged leather clothing with studded gauntlets.

"We finally meet at last!" he grins. "You're here to try and put an end to my existence, are you not? As if I really need an answer. Let us instead waste no more time with idle talk and begin combat, for there is no one who can pose a threat to my unconquerable might."

Advancing towards you, Gardav does not hold a physical weapon although you're about to learn that he tends to rely solely on his brutish physique. There are only seconds before this tyrant will be upon you for battle. Do you have a potential item to unleash on him? If so, now would be the best time to use it!

If you've got a crystal and think it might work, turn to **16**
If you would like to uncork a potion of rust, turn to **28**
If you reach for a pouch of shroud mist, turn to **37**
If you are in possession of a smoke ball, turn to **65**
If you have none of these, turn to **79**

93

Walking along this stretch of tunnel leads to a corner with water gushing down one side of the wall into a crack in the ground below. Next to this stands a dark-haired woman clad head to toe in jet black who doesn't say anything whatsoever as you cautiously approach her. Do you:

Reach for your sword in order to fight?	Turn to **14**
Try talking to the woman?	Turn to **25**
Ignore her completely?	Turn to **38**

94

You make your way along this new passage before finding yourself at another intersection. As you spend a moment to inspect each of the tunnels which lead off from here, one of them appears to have something that could possibly be of interest so you decide to head towards this direction in order to take a closer look.
Turn to **75**

95

There is no other option but to make an attempt to run for your life. Placing your sword back into its scabbard, you pause and take a massive breath. Then without further ado, you charge forward and dash past the mysterious shadow whilst it lashes out at you with its own razor-sharp weapon. Not daring to turn your head around for a split second whilst you hurriedly run for many metres, eventually you decide to stop and find that the shadow has not followed you in pursuit. It's only then you get the worrying sensation of something trickling down your arm, and upon glancing down you are extremely horrified to discover that you are severely bleeding. From what you previously saw it looked as if the shadow did not have a physical appearance, but the damage it has managed to inflict on you is most certainly real. Roll one die and lose that many VITALITY points. Should you still be alive, you frantically bandage the wound on your arm before it gets worse. Afterwards, you shakily continue your way along this tunnel which you hope leads to a less problematic area contained within these mines.
Turn to **50**

96

Arriving at another junction, one path continues ahead with an alternative option tailing off from the right.
To keep going forward, turn to **7**
To go for the right-hand path, turn to **54**

97

Drawing your sword, you get ready to do battle with the gargantuan beast as it prepares to strike down at you with its terrifying claws:

KRUDORFF
BRUTALITY 8 VITALITY 10

If you win, turn to **81**

98

You are satisfied that you've gained enough from Ornitram's quarters, and therefore leave to continue down the tunnel once again.
Turn to **86**

99

The ordeal of traversing the stepping stones becomes too much for you. Very nearly at the other side of the bank, you then take a poorly executed jump into the water instead of ending up where you intended to land. Swept downstream by the fast current, you lose consciousness and will be easy pickings for the flesh-eating monster who is lying in wait…
Your adventure ends here.

100

By the time you have escaped the Ordno Mines, the sun is rising and soon a new morning will have arrived where the people of Mottinghurst will no longer have to live in fear of the Ultraviolator. When you eventually arrive back at the village, you find Alton Sagar and inform him of this news. He immediately sends a group of people to secure the mines so it doesn't get ruled by another oppressor whilst freeing anyone who might have previously been kept prisoner. Deservedly you're then commended on your success and rewards of plenty will now be bestowed on you.

SPIRITUAL SACRILEGE

SPIRITUAL SACRILEGE

Introduction

The monks of Northgate Abbey are a group of quiet but friendly natured people who carry out their day-to-day activities without disturbance in their peaceful surroundings.

When they go to their neighbouring village of Darenthston, the monks supply needy residents with gifts of food and offer prayer for whatever difficulties people may be experiencing. It is also within the monk's code to offer shelter inside their abbey to anyone who desperately requires a place to stay.

Unfortunately, the latter would proceed to create unwelcome events in the abbey's surroundings. Not long ago, the village was visited by someone claiming to be a Myersian druid who had fled Xamalstad and was asking for somewhere to rest for a while before making the passage back home.

Believing his story, the monks offered to accommodate him so that he could fully recover. Only days later however, the so-called druid had infiltrated the main area of worship within the abbey before sealing it off from everyone else. Alas it was then this mysterious person's identity became revealed to the horror of the monks he had deceived…

This person was in fact the dark priest Kethnick of Holborus, who had been exiled from numerous lands for practising the methods of his evil arts. But now he has acquired somewhere else to restart his malice and summon a horde of ghastly entities into his realm within the abbey. Such is the threat of Kethnick that he must be stopped by whatever means; banishment from Northgate Abbey is in everyone's best interests yet a permanent end to his undesirable occultism is even more favourable.

Abbot Markenna, the leader of Northgate Abbey, wastes no time instructing one of his monks to go and find a trusty warrior that has a reputation of dealing with unwanted characters who have an intention of causing harm and destruction; these people in question need to be stopped before it's too late. The warrior Abbot Markenna has in mind is none other than you…

Brother Oakry is the monk tasked to locate your precise whereabouts; coincidentally he just happens to have also been previously trained to be an expert tracker. Within a matter of hours, he has come across you sitting on a bench located in one of the more peaceful outskirts of Falconleas Wood. It is here where you enjoy taking a moment to reflect upon your most recent missions which have resulted in success, with your sword unsheathed from its scabbard and resting upright in the soft earthly ground. Your silence is interrupted as the sound of Brother Oakry's footsteps advances towards your direction.

"Greetings!" says the monk upon joining you at the bench. "If you are willing, your services are required by myself and my fellow brethren at Northgate Abbey."

You nod in acknowledgement then look to Brother Oakry, asking him what needs to be done.

"Our usually peaceful dwelling has been sieged by the dark priest Kethnick, and my abbot has sent me to reach out to you. He believes that you are the only one right now who is capable enough of putting an end to the evil of this malignant egomaniac. As we speak, Kethnick has already begun to summon his immoral accomplices into the abbey via a portal he has created; it is necessary to cease what he has lined up before his powers infiltrate not just Darenthston, but who knows where else. Will you be the one to aid us?"

Knowing of the powers Kethnick possesses from a previous adventure, you come to the decision that this time he must indeed be stopped once and for all. Without hesitation, you inform Brother Oakry that you will be the one to rid Northgate Abbey of this dark priest.

A faint smile appears on the face of the monk as you inform him of your decision, before he stands up and turns around to make the return journey to Northgate Abbey with you at his side.

Nightfall has already set in by the time you both get there, and Brother Oakry takes you to Abbot Markenna who looks very relieved upon witnessing your arrival. The abbot greets you then asks to follow him to his chamber, where over a simple meal he speaks of the grim machinations already worked up by Kethnick within the main area of worship. After finishing your meal, the moment has come for you to prepare your initial course of action…

Now turn to **1**

1

As you ready your sword and sling your backpack over your shoulders, one of the abbey's chefs enters the chamber and gives you three food parcels to eat during this adventure. You thank them and are about to make your way when Abbot Markenna coughs to interrupt you.

"Perhaps I can give an additional item to be of assistance?" he suggests, as he walks over to a small cupboard situated on the lower wall of this chamber.

If you accept his offer and see what he provides, turn to **22**

If you say that you must get to Kethnick as soon as possible, turn to **35**

2

The corridor soon leads to a giant wooden door in the side of one wall. Glancing ahead, you are convinced that continuing down the corridor would lead back to where you started and this door you've come to must be the route to get further into the abbey. You turn the door's iron ring handle, and then enter a short brickwork passage with a similar door at the opposite end. As you make your way down this passage, you notice that in place of one of the bricks is a brass plaque. There appears to be some writing etched into it, but a thick layer of dirt covering the majority of the plaque means that whatever has been written on to it is currently illegible.

If you want to see what the plaque says, turn to **46**

If you ignore it and keep on walking, turn to **71**

3

Your final blow smashes into the skeleton with some devastating force, which causes it to fall apart and crash all over the floor. What was previously a skeletal creature summoned to do the bidding of Kethnick is now just a strewn heap of bones. Trying not to kick any of them as you step past, you then make your way down the rest of the passage.

Turn to **90**

4
If you possess a silver dagger, turn to **53**
If not, turn to **82**

5
The monk remains silent as you sit to join him at the table. Deciding that a simple verbal greeting may not be the best method to prompt a response, instead you try to come up with a question that will get the monk to react somehow. What will you ask him?
"Who are you?"   Turn to **26**
"How do I defeat Kethnick?"   Turn to **42**
"What is the safest passage?"   Turn to **78**

6
You rush to the aid of the cooks and shield them from any forthcoming attacks from the zombie. This creature groans as it advances and you are determined not to let it gorge on the flesh or brains of anyone else within its nearby vicinity. What approach will you use in order to attack it?
If you have a vial of holy water, turn to **28**
If not, turn to **44**

7
There is some caution as you unclench the dead warrior's fist to remove the spear, but upon grasping the weapon into your own hand before pulling it away nothing happens. Fortunately, the warrior remains still as you close the lid back on their coffin. You then admire the glowing spear whose silver alloys shine brightly next to where you stand. Note that you now have the spear amongst your possessions. Taking it with you, what will be your next move?
Examine the second coffin.   Turn to **50**
Or take a look at the third coffin.   Turn to **57**
If you decide there is nothing else worth investigating here, then it is time for you to move on. Turn to **83**

8

Explaining that you mean no harm and are here to dispose the abbey of Kethnick's unwarranted presence, the man backs down and his glowing ball of light vanishes.

"Ah yes, I was informed by Abbot Markenna that someone would be dealing with this!" he says in a serious tone. "Please excuse my initial concern. I don't know what strangers to trust ever since that damned rogue priest made himself unwelcome in our abbey. I am Father Bambrand, one of the genuine priests who have dwelled here for a number of years. It seems that you are indeed prepared to pit your wits against this malevolent being. Would you be so kind as to let me work something into your sword?"

You gently nod and take your sword out before handing it to Father Bambrand. He carefully holds the blade with both hands and utters some odd words that you cannot make out. After a few minutes, he returns the sword back to you.

"You should now be in a more advantageous position to take on Kethnick's power!" he informs you in a more calm, likeable manner. Bambrand goes on to state that he has blessed your sword and offers a plate of delicious meats alongside a cup filled with refreshing juice. Accepting both of these, you delightfully consume this nourishing meal. Restore 4 VITALITY points.

"Now you must continue directly along this passage", he explains. "Good luck, for Kethnick is not much further."

Thanking Bambrand for what he has done, you follow his instructions and leave to head via the instructed direction.
Turn to **94**

9

With your sword at the ready, the flying books aim down as you thought they would do. They are too many of them surrounding you however, and some of the books are such huge weighty tomes that they cause some damage upon hitting you. Lose 2 VITALITY points. If you are still alive, you decide to escape from the library before you are struck by more books. At least the door you entered by is still open and you slam it shut once you have returned to the hallway. You take a moment to look at some of the bruises inflicted by the books on to your skin before continuing onwards.
Turn to **76**

10

Leaving the chamber, you emerge into a corridor that stretches from east to west. Both ends of this corridor look identical in appearance, so which direction will you take?
To follow the west corridor, turn to **54**
Or to see what the east corridor may hold, turn to **87**

11

You get down to the ground as fast as you can and the skull flies past above your head without making any contact. Sensing that Kethnick is starting to become aware of your presence, you stand up then walk down the corridor without haste should the skull return for a second attack.
Turn to **49**

12

With the zombie defeated, your face the gracious cooks who are delighted that you've saved them. Being more cautious of what lies ahead though, you warn that they cannot rest until the person responsible has been vanquished for good. Despite that, the cooks try to remain upbeat and insist on giving you some of their freshly made stew. Accepting their gratitude of food, you tuck into this delicious hearty bowl. Restore 4 VITALITY points if previously wounded. Afterwards, the cooks wish you good luck for the rest of your adventure as you depart from the kitchen and walk down the corridor once again.
Turn to **36**

13

Looking down from the entrance of the crypt, you see that it is completely dark and no inclination as to what might be lying in wait down there. Some source of light will be needed should you wish to venture into the crypt to see what it holds. Alas, the torches on the wall are all securely attached with metal brackets and you won't be able to remove them.
If you have a lantern, turn to **41**
If not, turn to **75**

14

You open the vial and pour the entire contents of holy water into the coffin which dissipates the ghoul as if it were acid. Screaming in agony, the ghoul flails it arms but you are not one that wishes to see its demise. Hurriedly you close the lid back on the ghoul's coffin as its final wails can be heard whilst you ensure the lid is reattached. Once that's done, it is time to contemplate your next decision.
If you go over to the first coffin, turn to **29**
To see what might be in the third coffin, turn to **57**
However, it might be you've had enough of the coffins or already seen what they hold. In either case, turn to **83**

15

Making progress along this new location, you head down a long tunnel which continues down some stairs. At the bottom of the stairs is a new passage which you follow as it turns sharply to the right. Navigating the turn, you then come across a skeleton advancing forwards with a sword gripped in its left hand. This is another foe brought in by Kethnick and you must fight it if you are to progress. Note that as you do not carry a blunt weapon, you will only inflict 1 point of VITALITY damage each time you wound the skeleton.

SKELETON
BRUTALITY 7 VITALITY 5

If you win, turn to **3**

16

You light up the lantern using a torch on the wall before treading into the room to find out what lurks within. It takes only seconds after you've walked into the room for the door to slam shut behind you and the flame in your lantern to be extinguished completely. Then you hear some slight whirring, windy sounds as you are trapped in the darkness. All of a sudden, unseen shadowy spirits are entering your body to consume your entire soul and there is nothing you can do to prevent this from happening. No one else can stop Kethnick now, with the only person that was able to do so having been dispatched in the most sinister of circumstances. Your adventure ends here.

17

The door opens and you walk into a scene of delirium with half a dozen cooks fleeing in panic. A zombie has infiltrated their kitchen and is advancing towards them, with the intention of turning the innocent cooks of the monastery into fellow braindead servants!
If you attack the zombie, turn to **6**
If you back out and close the door, turn to **92**

18

You make your way down the long, rectangular formed corridor that soon widens out into an open area which has three coffins: one resting on the left-hand wall, another centred on the ground and the third leaning up against the right-hand wall. The chilling air surrounding them makes you feel uneasy and not wanting to linger in making a decision. Which of the coffins do you wish to have a look at?
The first coffin. Turn to **29**
The second coffin. Turn to **50**
The third coffin. Turn to **57**
Or if you would prefer not to investigate any of the coffins, turn to **83**

19
The monk suddenly gets up and walks towards the door where you entered, where he then opens it and points towards the hallway. It feels like he has had enough of you disturbing his silence and is now gesturing for you to leave. You will get no help from the monk and standing up with a hint of sadness, do as instructed. Leaving the room behind, you re-enter the hallway to find out what may lie beyond one of the other doors.
Turn to **60**

20
The damage inflicted by the wight has a particularly draining effect which causes part of your inner self to ebb away, making you feel less confident. Lose 1 BRUTALITY point. Continue fighting the wight and if you win, turn to **45**

21
You examine the shelves and pick out one book named *Distractions*. By some coincidence, that is exactly what happens next as a number of books start to fly off other shelves and hover around menacingly in the air above you! None of the books are swooping down to attack but you can't help and wonder what mystical force is animating them all. That said, you feel inclined to take some kind of action.
If you draw your sword, turn to **9**
If you stand your ground and speak, turn to **58**

22
Abbot Markenna smiles as he opens the cupboard.
"Resources are somewhat tight in the abbey and I can only let you have one of the following items." he says. What will you go for?

A lantern.	Turn to **48**
A silver dagger.	Turn to **61**
A vial of holy water.	Turn to **74**

23

As soon as he sees you draw your sword, the man flings the glowing ball of white light at you.

"Fool!" he rages. "You will be taught to think twice before attempting to attack a man of the holy order!" The light hits its target and you are immediately frozen to the spot. Having attempted to do battle with this man you've encountered, what you didn't realise is that he is one of Northgate Abbey's highly skilled priests who are well versed to deal with anyone who presents themselves as hostile towards them. However, as Kethnick entered the abbey in disguise he was able to slip in unnoticed before being able to shield himself from any retaliation to the macabre work he began to perform. You will eventually become free from the spell that has you fixed where you are standing, but by then Kethnick's plans will have got fully underway and it will be too late. Your adventure ends here.

24

The cooks are eternally grateful to you for saving them from the threat of the zombie. You hesitate and point out that their lives are still at risk until Kethnick has been defeated. Nonetheless, they insist on keeping you pepped up for the rest of the adventure and provide a freshly made stew for you to eat. Restore 4 VITALITY points if previously wounded. Your vial of holy water is also refilled for another use, so you don't need to remove it from your adventure sheet just yet. Once again you are thanked by the cooks as they bid you good luck for the rest of your adventure. Leaving the kitchen, you set off back down the corridor.
Turn to **36**

25

Intrigued as to where the new path might lead, you head along the passage which eventually leads to some stairs leading upwards. Walking up them, you reach the top and your heart sinks as it emerges you have come to a dead end. About to retreat to where you were previously, an arrow suddenly thuds into your back causing you to slump face down on to the ground. You pass out and do not witness the assassin sent by Kethnick race up the stairs to finish you off. Now you're out of the way, no one else can put a stop to the malicious plans of the dark priest. Your adventure ends here.

26

The monk looks at you blankly. It seems that who he is or what he does is none of your concern. Attempting another question, what will you now ask him?

"How do I defeat Kethnick?" Turn to **19**
"What is the safest passage?" Turn to **78**

27

Turning the handle, you push the door open which leads into the nave of the monastery. At the far end is the sanctuary, which contains the altar and standing in front of it is none other than Kethnick himself. The dark priest having seen you enter, walks down the nave in order for a confrontation.

"So, this is the one who's been sent to put an end to my works!" he grins. "Too bad you don't realise the full extent of the power I behold. Allow me to demonstrate…"

Kethnick pulls out a large ceremonial knife that is obsidian in colour with red runes carved into the blade. He shows no fear as he advances towards the place where you stand. Defying his taunts to ready yourself in defence, what will you use against him?

A silver dagger. Turn to **38**
A spear. Turn to **59**
A sword. Turn to **66**

28
You uncork the vial and hurl its contents towards the advancing zombie. Roll two dice.
If it's less than or equal to your PHYSICALITY, turn to **63**
If the total is greater than your PHYSICALITY, turn to **79**

29
You go over to the coffin so that you can prise it wide open. The lid comes off and inside lies the body of a long dead warrior still in their battle armour, holding a silver spear which doesn't appear to have rotted or decayed whatsoever.
If you attempt to take the spear, turn to **7**
If you leave the spear where it is, turn to **98**

30
You turn the hands of the clock to the time specified by the parchment. The clock then clicks and you push it backwards to find a new passage leading from here. With nowhere else to go, you follow the newly found passage where it turns and leads down some steps. Eventually you come to a junction; looking at the right-hand path you see that it has steps leading back upwards and conclude that this will return you to a part of the monastery you have previously visited. Instead, you opt for the flattened floor of the left-hand path hoping it will reach somewhere you haven't been to yet.
Turn to **86**

31

You enter a finely decorated room with colourful paintings and lush tapestries of various sizes adorning its walls. In the centre of the room sits a monk by a table with an empty chair opposite him. The monk's hood covers the whole of his face so you cannot recognise him, and his hands are also concealed by the length of his tunic. He doesn't appear to acknowledge that you have entered the room either.
If you try talking to the monk, turn to **5**
If you'd rather fight him, turn to **84**

32

"This is a very simple one to learn." smiles Pendrell. "If the cross consists of a vertical and horizontal line, then you can be assured that a holy member of the monastery resides there. If the lines of the cross are both diagonal however, then what awaits you beyond that cross is deathly and must be avoided at all costs."
Turn to **80**

33

The crypt may not look appealing, but you avert your focus away from the skulls and advance towards the table. Holding your lantern above the parchment, you read what it says:

The time of impending doom is upon us.
There may be an occasion when we deal with time itself.
The face of time should be twenty minutes past ten.
That is the correct time to escape.

There is nothing else of interest within the crypt, so you ascend back up the steps. You have safely made your way out of the crypt when the lantern's flame extinguishes, meaning you'll have to discard it. Cross the lantern off your list of items before returning to walk along the corridor.
Turn to **2**

34
You walk into the room clearly unprepared for what's going to happen next. As you become shrouded by darkness, the door behind you slams shut and you're defenceless as shadowy spirits drift into your body to drain whatever life is inside you. Now that you're out of the way, Kethnick is free to unleash the vast legions of chaos he has been summoning. Your adventure ends here.

35
"Very well!" says the abbot. "You seem to recognise the urgency of this mission, so I shall advise to seek out our librarian as he knows a safe route through our monastery."
Thanking the abbot, you state that you'll do whatever it takes to defeat Kethnick before making your exit.
Turn to **10**

36
Proceeding along the corridor, you come to another turn and follow the new path. Surprisingly, you are untroubled as this passageway feels eerily silent. No doubt though Kethnick has something lined up deeper within the monastery…
Turn to **2**

37

Pulling down on the handle, you enter what appears to be a darkened office. A solitary small candle burns in one corner of this room, and in the centre is a worn-out desk that looks as if it has been well ravaged. All of a sudden you hear a moaning sound come from another corner, and you look to see a figure concealed by the darkness standing next to another door. Then the figure slowly advances towards you, with the light from the candle eventually revealing the full horror of what it is. Pale white skin is partially covered by ripped rags, with a rotting soft armour barely protecting its torso. Deathly clawed hands then start to reach out to attack you. The figure in this room is none other than a wight!
If you fight this creature, turn to **4**
If you'd rather attempt to flee from its clutches, turn to **69**

38

You grab hold of the dagger and point it towards Kethnick. Whilst it is indeed made of the finest silver, alas that does not mean it is magical in nature for these are the only weapons that can harm the dark priest. Kethnick responds by walking undaunted over to you and plunging his ceremonial knife into your heart. Falling agonisingly at the final encounter, your last visions are of the dark priest returning to the altar. There is no one who'll be able to stop him now. Your adventure ends here.

39

Walking through the door, you find yourself heading down another passage where you soon come to two doors directly opposite one another. The door on the left has the symbol + on the front, and the door on the right bears the symbol ×. Do you think that either of these are worth investigating?
To go through the door labelled +, turn to **52**
To see what is through the door marked ×, turn to **73**
Or if you choose to ignore both doors, turn to **94**

40

Opening the coffin, you are immediately sucked into the black vortex situated inside. There is no escape and you are doomed to spend the rest of eternity falling through a darkened void. Kethinck will no doubt take great pleasure in learning you fell into this trap. Your adventure ends here.

41

Using the wick inside the lantern, you hold it up against one of the flaming steel torches which ignites the lantern's oil almost immediately. Next you close the lantern door and hold up your flickering light as you advance down the steps of the crypt. Once at the bottom, you look around where your lantern reveals a parchment on a wooden table as well as some very macabre looking skulls which are lined up along the crypt's shelves. Roll two dice.
If it's less than or equal to your MENTALITY, turn to **33**
If the total is greater than your MENTALITY, turn to **67**

42

Your question does not prompt a reaction from the monk. Despite what Kethnick is doing inside the monastery, this matter appears to be of no interest to the monk who sits before you. Perplexed but not put off from asking him something else, what will you question the monk with now?
"Who are you?" Turn to **19**
"What is the safest passage?" Turn to **78**

43

You open the door and walk into what looks to be a library. Every wall is adorned by shelves that are filled to the edges with books, some appear to be very worn with others looking to have a wealth of information inside them.
If you would like to read some of the books, turn to **21**
If you'd rather leave instead and continue down the hallway, turn to **76**

44

Drawing your sword, you are ready to fight the zombie as it reaches out with its bare hands to attack you.

ZOMBIE
BRUTALITY 6 VITALITY 6

If you win, turn to **12**

45

The wight falls at last. You tuck the silver dagger back into your belt and investigate the room you're in, but find nothing of value. Switching your attention to the door located at the opposite end, you walk over to open it and discover a flight of stairs leading down to another section of the monastery.
If you would like to see where these stairs lead, turn to **77**
Otherwise, you return back to the hallway. Turn to **88**

46

You look at the plaque and brush off the dirt with just one swipe of your hand. The words on the plaque read as follows:

"Don't go to the end if you don't know the time."

Curious as to what it means, you note this sentence before taking the few paces required to get to the end of the passage. Turn to **95**

47

Your final blow of the sword cuts deep into Kethnick who screams with rage as a dazzling light source emerges from your blade and consumes the whole of the dark priest. Shielding your eyes momentarily, you then look around to find that Kethnick no longer has a presence within the nave. He has been vanquished once and for all.
Turn to **100**

48

The lantern comes with a wick and enough oil for one use; make a note of this on your Adventure Sheet. You thank the abbot and vow that you'll do whatever it takes to defeat Kethnick before leaving the chamber to commence your adventure.
Turn to **10**

49

The first door you come to on the left-hand wall is fairly simple looking compared to some of the others you've previously seen in this monastery. It is small but very sturdy, with a shiny metallic handle that will open it upon being pulled down.
If you investigate what's beyond this door, turn to **31**
If you decide to ignore it and continue down the hallway, turn to **60**

50

You kneel down at the coffin which lies before you and lift up the lid. It only takes a matter of seconds afterwards for a gruesome hand to claw out at you and in alarming disgust, your response is to flinch back in horror at its repulsiveness! Roll two dice.
If it's less than or equal to your MENTALITY, turn to **81**
If the total is greater than your MENTALITY, turn to **93**

51

Searching the lifeless body of the assassin, you don't find anything in his possession that could be of use. All you do know is that Kethnick must be wary you're somewhere nearby, and is now doing everything he can to halt your progress. Feeling even more determined to get to him than ever before, you continue to walk down the passage with a suspicion that the dark priest can't be too far away.
Turn to **90**

52

Walking through the door, you go into a room that is reminiscent of a study. A man in a white robe who is busy working at a table glances up upon hearing you enter and gives a scrutinising look that is none too happy for disturbing whatever he was up to.

"Who are you?" he demands. "Speak now, or you'll instantly regret interrupting me during a crucial moment of extremely high importance!"

A fizzing ball of white light begins to sparkle in his hand. You'll have to think without hesitation if you are to avoid the wrath of this man!

If you say who you are, turn to **8**
If you draw your sword in defence, turn to **23**
If you apologise and leave, turn to **94**

53

Your past experiences have taught you that wights can only be damaged by magical or silver weapons. With this in mind, you get the dagger out before the creature you're facing can get an advantage. Now feeling more prepared to take on the wight, this could still be a difficult battle:

WIGHT
BRUTALITY 8 VITALITY 6

If the wight wounds you three times, turn to **20**
If you win without this occurring, turn to **45**

54

You make your way along and notice a door set into the wall just as the corridor takes a sharp turn. There are no sounds being made from the other side when you approach the door to investigate.

If you open the door, turn to **17**
If you would rather keep on walking, turn to **89**

55
The ghoul paralyses you! Unable to move from where you're standing, all you can do is remain firm as the ghoul starts to feast on your body. It literally makes a meal out of you, and any chances of Kethnick's devious intentions being put to a halt are also swallowed up. Your adventure ends here.

56
Deciding that urgency is important without the need to search every nook and cranny of the monastery, you bypass the crypt entrance in the hope that you can reach Kethnick sooner rather than later. You continue down the corridor when it eventually bends round to the left.
Turn to **2**

57
You go over to the coffin by the right-hand wall. Once there, you notice that it has a pentagram etched on to its lid.
If you go ahead and open it, turn to **40**
If you decide against opening the coffin, turn to **68**

58

You stay firm and shout that you mean no harm, having come to dispose the monastery of Kethnick. The books slowly float back to where they previously were before and then in front of you appears an old man with a look of great wisdom about him. A pair of circular spectacles are arched on the nose of his face and he wears a long light brown coloured robe with a rope tied around his waist.

"Excuse me for what you just witnessed!" he says politely. "One can't be too careful ever since the arrival of this Kethnick character; such has been the devastation he's already caused that certain residents including myself have had to resort to using cloaks of invisibility in order to ensure they keep as well protected as is possibly deemed. I must confess that Abbot Markenna informed me you were due to come to the monastery, and if your intention is to eradicate our dark priest then I'm all for offering my assistance. My name is Pendrell and I am the monastery's librarian. I'm afraid I cannot weald a sword or use any weapon in combat, but perhaps I might be able to help in another form or two."

Following Pendrell to where he reveals a previously hidden table in the corner of the library, you find there is a large plate of bread. He offers it to you which you accept and eat. Regain 4 VITALITY points if you were previously wounded. Next, Pendrell looks up to the shelves to peruse some books. "As time is very precious, I can only teach you one of these subjects", he indicates. "A few records kept over the past centuries have the capability to provide you with some knowledge of expectations within the deeper parts of the monastery, so what would you like to learn about?"

Three of the books are pulled out from the shelves by Pendrell with different one-word subjects on each of their covers. Which do you think will be the most beneficial?

Crosses.	Turn to **32**
Pentagrams.	Turn to **64**
Shapes.	Turn to **96**

59

In a manner which can somewhat be described as presumptuous, Kethnick has unwittingly not taken into consideration the almighty power of the spear you are holding. It is a weapon that previously belonged to the Andrad Templars, a group of legendary knights who were specially equipped to overcome dark sorcery that had tainted many lands of earlier centuries and the warrior you took this spear from in fact happened to be one of those very knights. Brandishing the spear, you wield it in the direction of the dark priest as you get ready to take him on for an ultimate fight to the finish:

KETHNICK
BRUTALITY 9 VITALITY 12

If you win, turn to **72**

60

Not long afterwards, you arrive at another door which this time happens to be situated in the right-hand wall. Appearance wise, this door looks exactly the same as the one which you encountered on the opposite side a matter of moments ago.
If you look to see what's beyond this door, turn to **37**
If you keep on walking down the hallway instead, turn to **88**

61

The silver dagger has a sharp blade and looks to be very well crafted upon examination.
"It's especially useful against creatures that can't be harmed by normal weapons!" hints the abbot. You thank him for the assistance he has provided and swear that you'll defeat Kethnick before leaving the chamber so that your adventure can get underway.
Turn to **10**

62

You are not swift enough as the skull flies through where you stand. Whilst it only lasts seconds, the aftershock of this spectral apparition entering then exiting your body with incredible ease causes a previously unknown trauma within you. Lose 1 BRUTALITY and 1 MENTALITY point. Feeling shaken at how the flying skull has drained your energy in the way it has, there is a suspicion that Kethnick is aware of your presence and getting ready to summon more frightful entities who can do his bidding. Hurriedly you rush down the hallway in case the flying skull makes an unwelcome return.
Turn to **49**

63

The vial hits the zombie and the holy water spills out, splashing all over the undead creature's limbs. Wailing in a moan of agony, the zombie falls to the ground and then becomes a lifeless corpse where it will no longer trouble anyone. You then focus your attention on the cooks who look very relieved after what you've accomplished.
Turn to **24**

64

"Beware of anything that happens to show the mark of a pentagram!" warns Pendrell. "If you come across the sign of a star within a circle, this contains all the warnings of an unspeakable fate. And we wouldn't want such a thing to be happening to you now…"
Turn to **80**

65

You are able to hit the wight a second time with your sword, but once again the creature does not sustain any damage. Pausing in disbelief, you try to figure out what is going on when the wight manages to seize the initiative and uses its hand to claw deep into your stomach. As you worriedly look downwards to see your blood gushing out where it has attacked you, the wight gets another opportunity to strike again but this time it aims higher and slashes your neck. More blood pours on to your garments as you fall to the ground due to the severity of your wounds, defenceless as the vile lusus naturae gets to finish you off mercilessly. Failing to realise that the wight is only vulnerable to magic or silver weapons, it is now too late for anyone else to prevent Kethnick from bringing forth more undead beings to carry out his ill-natured plans. Your adventure ends here.

66

Has your sword been blessed during this adventure?
If it has, turn to **85**
If not, turn to **99**

67

All of a sudden nearly every skull in the crypt bursts into life, with those who still have two rows of teeth chattering them furiously. The horrid clacking sound they make becomes too unbearable for you to handle, and as fast as possible you race back up the steps then out of the crypt to avoid listening to them any more than you have to. Once you have regained your composure in the safety of the corridor, you find that your lantern's flame has been extinguished and you must now remove it from your list of items. Regretting this unfortunate recent encounter, you continue along the corridor once again whilst trying to forget about what happened at the crypt.
Turn to **2**

68

You decide not to spend any time looking in this coffin and plan on what to do next.
To check out the first coffin, turn to **29**
Or to examine the second coffin, turn to **50**
If you've been to all the coffins (or had enough), turn to **83**

69

You spin round and desperately try to flee out of the room, but in doing so the wight's needle-like claws rake your back. Lose 2 VITALITY points. If you are still alive, you hurriedly dash out of the room but the wight does not give chase. Instead, it prefers to stay within its existing dark confines. With a thankful breath of relief that the damage you took wasn't any more serious, you proceed to continue back down the hallway.
Turn to **88**

70

The ghoul staggers and reels back before finally collapsing on to the side of its coffin. Almost inclined to put it back in there as well as permanently sealing the lid, you instead decide to contemplate on what you believe to be more important matters.
If you want to see what might be lurking in the first coffin, turn to **29**
To investigate the third coffin, turn to **57**
Or if you've simply had enough of looking inside the coffins (or been to them all), turn to **83**

71

Uninterested as to what might be written beneath the thickened dirt that happens to grace the plaque, you continue onwards and after a while reach the wooden door at the other end of the passage.
Turn to **95**

72
The spear impales itself into Kethnick's heart, as with one final lunge you overcome him with the decisive blow. Next, a blinding white light fills the nave and using one arm to shield your eyes the dark priest's screams of rage surround the area you are standing. Once both the light and Kethnick's last yells have subsided, you look around to find that the monastery has no trace whatsoever of the dark priest having ever been there. Noticing that the spear you were fighting with has gone too, you conclude that it was taken at the same moment Kethnick was removed from this world.
Turn to **100**

73
The door opens and peering inside reveals that it leads into a room which is completely shrouded in mysterious darkness. You cannot make out anything which could be inside there, nor can you hear the sounds of whatever it is that might be lurking in wait.
If you have a lantern which you could possibly use to explore, turn to **16**
If you don't have a lantern but decide to go into the room anyway, turn to **34**
If you choose not to go into the room but would like to have a look at the door marked + if you haven't already done so, turn to **52**
If you opt to leave both doors behind, turn to **94**

74
The vial contains enough holy water for the fulfilment of one use only, but as Abbot Markenna points out it is very effective against any undead beings you might happen to encounter within the monastery. You thank the abbot and promise to defeat Kethnick before leaving the chamber to begin your adventure.
Turn to **10**

75
The lack of a portable light means you won't be able to go inside the crypt safely. Leaving it behind, you take the only option available by continuing down the corridor.
Turn to **2**

76
It is not long before you have reached the end of the hallway. There are no more doors here, but what is in front of you is a giant analogue clock whose hands seem to be completely dormant. You put one ear next to the clock and it is not ticking. The clock is not functioning whatsoever. Although it does have both its large hand and small hand, so perhaps you might be able to set it to a precise time in order to find out what happens? If you know what time to set the clock, add together the numbers involved and turn to the section which is the same as the number of your answer. Should the number you turn to make no sense, or you don't know what time to set the clock then you must turn to **91**

77
You tread down the steps with caution in preparation for anything that might attack unexpectedly. To your relief however, nothing happens as you make it down to the bottom. Walking along the passage which follows, you soon come to a junction with a new path branching off to the left.
If you see where this path might take you, turn to **25**
If you prefer to keep going straight onwards, turn to **86**

78

You put the question to the monk who stands up and walks towards a long hanging tapestry in one corner of the room. Pulling it to one side, a doorway which was previously hiding behind the tapestry is now revealed before you and the monk indicates that this is the route to follow.

If you trust the monk's help and go through the doorway as he instructs, turn to **15**

If you're feeling uneasy about this new path, then you back out and leave the room via where you came in. Turn to **60**

79

The vial misses, gliding harmlessly above the zombie's head. You have no other option but to draw your sword and fight as the zombie attempts to lash out at you with its bare hands:

ZOMBIE
BRUTALITY 6 VITALITY 6

If you win, turn to **24**

80

Pendrell then gets up out of his seat to walk over to another corner of the library. He proceeds to pull out a book, which clicks and activates a mechanism to make the bookshelf rotate. Walking over to where he is standing, you find that a secret passageway has now made itself known.

"If you want to reach where Kethnick currently lies, then this is definitely the best way to go!" nods Pendrell. Already thankful for the assistance he has given you and deeming him to be trustworthy, you shake his hand before starting to walk down the passageway.

"Best of luck and I hope you dispose of that wretched Kethnick for us!" smiles Pendrell with a bout of enthusiasm as you keenly look as to where you'll end up next.
Turn to **15**

81

You do not allow yourself to be transfixed by what is trying to attack. Retreating to avoid the hand that is lashing out, you glance into the coffin and recoil at the foulness you've unleashed. For this is none other than a ghoul!

If you have a vial of holy water, you'd better use it now – turn to **14**

Otherwise, the ghoul pushes the coffin lid open and climbs out before advancing towards you. Drawing your sword, you get ready to fight this despicable creature:

GHOUL
BRUTALITY 7 VITALITY 6

If the ghoul wounds you three times, turn at once to **55**
If you win without taking this much damage, turn to **70**

82

You draw your sword before striking out at the wight.
The blade of your weapon makes contact but amazingly, your opponent comes off unscathed! Panic sets in as you fear that it could be protected by Kethnick. What will you do?
If you continue fighting the wight, turn to **65**
If you decide against this and make a run for it, turn to **97**

83

You leave the coffins and press along the corridor again. Suspicion arises that your current nemesis is near, and this is pretty much confirmed once arriving at an intersection. There's one path which looks as if it would lead backwards, but switching your attention to the other path reveals a huge door in the distance that's crafted unlike any other you've seen so far in this monastery. Walking over, you put one hand on the door and instantly you get the sensation that the person you're looking for is only a few more steps away…
Turn to **27**

84

You draw your sword and strike at the hooded monk. Incredibly though, upon being touched by the blade of your sword there is disbelief as the monk's tunic falls to the ground with absolutely no trace of him having ever been in the room! Perplexed, you reluctantly put your sword away and realise you will get no assistance here. You leave and continue back down the hallway.

Turn to **60**

85

Unsheathing your weapon, amazement beholds you as the sword's blade sparkles into life. Bambrand's influence has detected the presence of dark magic, and Kethnick hesitates as he senses what your weapon has become capable of. Nonetheless, he continues to approach with his ceremonial knife in hand and you respond by raising your blessed sword which now has the ability to inflict the necessary wounds on the dark priest. The monks of Northgate Abbey will be praying you can overcome this battle to the end:

KETHNICK
BRUTALITY 9 VITALITY 12

If you win, turn to **47**

86

You make your way onwards and follow the path which soon twists to the left. A few paces later and you make out a dark shape advancing towards you. Staying firm until you can make sure what it is, you eventually identify what is in fact a cloaked figure with its hood up and armed with a dagger! This character is none other than an assassin ordered by Kethnick to stop you in your tracks. You must fight:

ASSASSIN
BRUTALITY 7 VITALITY 6

If you win, turn to **51**

87

The corridor you're walking along is lit by steel torches fixed to the wall which guide you to the route that should be taken. As you turn round a corner, you soon come to a passageway with the word *Crypt* written above it.
If you investigate what might be inside, turn to **13**
If not, turn to **56**

88

Another wooden door emerges, this time on the left-hand side. Looking at the handle, you find that it is no different to the others you have previously walked past in this hallway.
If you choose to open this door, turn to **43**
If you ignore it and keep on walking, turn to **76**

89

You decide not to investigate what may lie beyond the door and instead proceed to keep walking onwards.
Turn to **36**

90

At the end of this passage the path opens up into a small area with two doors. You look at the doors and notice that above one of them is a rectangle, and above the other is a square.
To enter the door with a rectangle, turn to **18**
To head down the door with a square, turn to **39**

91

You do not know what to do at the clock, so turn back round to retrace your steps. That is when you see the ghastly flying skull return and on this occasion you're too late to respond. When the skull makes contact with you, it drains your remaining energy and you slump in a lifeless state to the ground. Kethnick's wraith-like entity has put a stop to your attempt at halting the commencement of the dark priest's sinister wave of terror. Your adventure ends here.

92

That was a callous move. These were the same cooks who made you food to eat during your adventure, and this is how you thank them? Leaving the unfortunate souls to a merciless fate of this rampaging zombie, you shamefully regret your decision and continue on your way.
Turn to **36**

93

You are so filled with intense dread at what you're seeing that it becomes completely impossible to move as the hand bursts out of the coffin to strike you directly in the chest. Lose 2 VITALITY points. If you are still alive, you regain composure just as the grim creature has fully risen out of the coffin and is climbing out to finish you off. Drawing your sword in defence, you prepare to fight this apparition which has revealed itself to be a ghoul!

GHOUL
BRUTALITY 7 VITALITY 6

If the ghoul wounds you twice, turn at once to **55**
If you win without this occurring, turn to **70**

94

Proceeding along the passage, you soon come to another intersection. Having a look at one of the paths, you conclude that it would reverse the progress you've made which isn't what you want to do. The other path however has a door in the distance which you make out to be bigger and grander in appearance than any other you've seen in the monastery. You walk up to the door and place one hand on it when an eerie sensation flows down from head to feet. Instantly you sense that the adversary you've been seeking is awaiting you on the other side…
Turn to **27**

95

You open the door and step into an elaborate hallway with doors leading off from either side. Without warning, a huge ghastly skull appears from the opposite end of the hallway and flies screeching towards you! As the skull continues to advance, instinctively you attempt to duck. Roll two dice.
If it's less than or equal to your PHYSICALITY, turn to **11**
If the total is greater than your PHYSICALITY, turn to **62**

96

"We use different shapes here in the monastery", says Pendrell. A rectangle leads to the abode of our dead, and a square will take you to our priest's study."
Turn to **80**

97

Turning round frantically in a desperate bid to escape, the wight retaliates by inflicting its claws at your exposed back. Lose 2 VITALITY points. If you are still alive, you manage to get out of the room and take a short moment to look behind you once certain that you've managed to get some distance away from this creature. The wight has not followed, as it would rather stay within its own darkened habitat. Gratefully sighing with relief, you place your sword back into its scabbard before proceeding to wander down the hallway once again.
Turn to **88**

98

You decide not to relieve the dead warrior of its spear and respectfully close the lid on its coffin. Once that it is done, you decide on what should be done next.
If you want to have a look at the second coffin, turn to **50**
If you see what the third coffin might hold, turn to **57**
If you've been to all the coffins (or rather leave them be), turn to **83**

99

Kethnick confidently spins his knife around as you draw your sword. Unknown to you, the dark priest has made himself immune to normal weapons and when you attempt to strike out at him, you find that no wounds appear on Kethnick's skin. Bewildered at what is happening, you're at sixes and sevens due to the confusion before you as he finally takes hold of the opportunity to plunge his ceremonial knife deep into your vital organs. As you're slumping to the ground, the look on your face is that of a puzzled expression. Whilst you were almost within an inch of thwarting the plans of this scheming dark priest, instead he is now free to commence the motions of his apocalyptic machinations. Your adventure ends here.

100

You turn around and find Abbot Markenna along with other members of the monastery approach towards you. They undoubtedly heard Kethnick's screams of defeat from elsewhere and wanted to make certain for themselves that he is no more. Nodding in their direction, you assure them that he will no longer trouble the monastery, or anyone else for that matter, ever again.

"We cannot thank you enough!" says Abbot Markenna as you walk towards him and the rest of the holy crowd. Next to the abbot stands Brother Oakry, who clasps your shoulder in acknowledgement of your victory. You join the monks in a celebratory banquet after any wounds you sustained have been tended to. Staying the night in the monastery, the following morning you go with the monks to Darenthston. When the people there learn of what you have accomplished, you will be guaranteed an even bigger celebration.

TORMENTOR TREETOWER

TORMENTOR TREETOWER

INTRODUCTION

You are an adventurer situated in Moordown, a village situated on the edge of Falconleas Wood. The nearby towns and villages have championed you for the accomplishments you have attained in putting an end to the threat of various evildoers who dare attempt to cause havoc across the land.

Over the years however, a strange being by the name of Thalkatar has made his unwelcome home at a previously desolate tower within Falconleas Wood. His acquired home is referred to as the Treetower as it is surrounded by a high density of trees. As for Thalkatar, he has brought with him an army of guards who capture anyone that dares make an approach to the tower. These unwitting victims would then be taken for torture at the hands of Thalkatar himself. Hence, he has inherited the name of "The Tormentor".

One day whilst you are in Moordown having a drink at the Invicta Tavern, one of the village's esteemed characters in Admiral Dunbreck bursts through the door exclaiming that one of his assistants has become the most recent capture of Thalkatar's henchmen. It is at this point where you decide to vow in putting an end to the Tormentor's tyranny.

Later that evening, you set off into Falconleas Wood using a map which has marked on it the exact location of the Treetower. Following Stoney Alley as far as Long Pond, eventually you find the pavement that's almost silhouetted in darkness. It is along this way you must tread and stealth is needed to avoid any guards if you're to safely arrive at the habitat of the despicable being who is being hunted down…

Now turn to **1**

1

You make your way along the shady lane and are soon within reach of the treetower itself. Despite its grave architecture, the treetower looks slanted and enchanted with tree branches covering all of its windows. Somewhere inside here lurks Thalkatar, and you are determined to put an end to the torment he has unleashed upon the good people of Falconleas Wood as well as its surrounding areas. Walking up to the treetower, you see that there appears to be only one entrance leading inside though there may be another means of entry on the other side should you wish to investigate.
If you go through the only visible door, turn to **28**
If you look for another way in, turn to **40**

2

The dwarf falls and does not get up again. Its days of launching rocks at unsuspecting adventurers are no more. Examining the warhammer, you find that it is crafted in a fashion which means that it can only be used by dwarfs. Being not too disappointed, you then walk up to the rocks. You may take some (up to a maximum of three) if you have a slingshot as they can restore any lost ammunition. There is also some meat, and you take a moment to sit down where you can enjoy this tasty food. Restore 4 VITALITY points. Once fully rested, you get back up to get the next phase of your adventure underway.
Turn to **79**

3

The beds here appear unoccupied, although you are intrigued by a dark shade which is lurking underneath the lower bunk.
If you look at the darkness, turn to **12**
Otherwise, you can either:
Opt to look at the bunk bed on the right.   Turn to **47**
Open the cupboard.   Turn to **59**
Or leave the room.   Turn to **64**

4

You go up to the barrels. There are four of them in total, and upon taking a closer inspection you notice that their lids will come off rather easily. Choose which barrel you would like to inspect:

The first barrel.	Turn to **17**
The second barrel.	Turn to **32**
The third barrel.	Turn to **48**
The fourth barrel.	Turn to **65**

5

You put the burning charcoal to the tree branch and within seconds you are in possession of your own flaming torch. Thalkatar begins to feel nervous at the prospect of what your newly acquired weapon could do to him, but he continues forward still determined to put an end to your existence. Wielding your torch, you need to hit Thalkatar only once to cause serious damage to the Tormentor. Battle him as if you were in a normal fight:

THALKATAR
BRUTALITY 9

If Thalkatar has the higher Attack Rating during a round of battle, he wounds you as normal.
If you ever have the higher Attack Rating though, the torch sets fire to Thalkatar and you step back as the flame on his body increases. He is soon burnt to a blackened ash, powerlessly beat. You extinguish the flame from your torch. Turn to **37**

6

You manage to compose yourself from the shock you've received, but are still disgusted by the sight of the corpse that you run out of the room and hurry back down the passage. Turn to **38**

7

"To get to the highest level of this tower where Thalkatar can be found, you will need to climb up some vines", explains Loretta. "Only the central vine will get you there safely, however. I hope that you will go on to defeat Thalkatar himself as I for one can't wait for the moment of his demise. Good luck!"

You thank Loretta for this advice and get up out of the chair to leave the room where you continue onwards.

Turn to **80**

8

You are unable to prevent yourself from being bitten by the serpent's fangs for a second time. Paralysed, your motionless body can only watch in horror as the serpent coils its body around you to feast on your flesh. Your adventure ends here.

9

You load the slingshot with one of the pebbles before running back up the stairs to fire at the dwarf. Roll two dice. If the total is less than or equal to your BRUTALITY then you have successfully hit the dwarf, in which case turn to **54** If the total is greater than your BRUTALITY, then you have missed. You retreat back down the stairs to safety and out of the dwarf's line of sight. Remember that you still have two pebbles remaining should you wish to fire these at the dwarf – if you choose to do so repeat the above process until you successfully hit it.

If all these pebbles miss (or you choose to save the remaining pebbles for later), then you have no option but to run the risk of braving it up the stairs.
Turn to **81**

10

Respecting the pixie's wishes, you close the lid back down on the barrel and leave it in peace. You may now open one of the other barrels if you haven't already done so:

The first barrel.	Turn to **17**
The second barrel.	Turn to **32**
The fourth barrel.	Turn to **65**

If you've had enough of looking into each of these barrels (or have already opened all of them), then turn to **90**

11

Wondering what is happening, you burst through the door to find an orc flogging a whimpering young man in chains! The man is shaking from the orc's attack and you wonder why he is being inflicted with such punishment. Should he suffer any more lashes from the flail, then it is highly unlikely that this man will be breathing for much longer. You feel the need to put a stop to this, but whose side will you choose?

If you defend the young man, turn to **25**
Or if you would rather assist the orc, turn to **44**

12
You peer underneath the lower bunk, curious as to what may be causing the darkness down there. Putting your head closely to the ground, a pair of red eyes suddenly appear in front of you and without warning an unseen force is wrapping itself around you in a stranglehold! This sinister power then drags you towards the red eyes where you feel your very soul being consumed. You have been trapped by a Shade Lurker, a creature which delights in preying on unaware victims in dark spaces and there is no chance for you to prevent it feeding on the last drips of your willpower. This adventure ends here.

13
You follow the path and eventually come to a slightly open door with a colourful glow emitting from the room inside.
If you like to find out what is causing the glow, turn to **26**
If you would rather press onwards, turn to **39**

14
You are inside the base of the treetower. Two passageways lead off from where you stand, though neither look inviting. Somehow you get the feeling that this is Thalkatar's preference. Choose which direction you would like to go!
If you head down the left-hand passageway, turn to **57**
If you follow the right-hand passageway instead, turn to **85**

15

The serpent is able to get itself into a rhythm when it can swing its tail to knock you off your feet. For a brief moment, you are unconscious but that gives the serpent enough time to gorge its fangs into your neck. Lose 6 VITALITY points. If you are still alive, you mutter that there is no way you're going to let this slippery enemy overcome you. Summoning the remaining energy in your body, you get up off the floor and finish the serpent before it can strike again.
Continue fighting the serpent as normal, but if it injures you again then you must turn at once to **8**
If you defeat the serpent without it inflicting any further damage upon yourself, turn to **70**

16

The liquid in the bottle is refreshing and you feel revitalised. In fact, you have just drunk a potion of strength and may restore your VITALITY to its score when you started this adventure. With a renewed sense of optimism, you decide to leave the room and stride confidently to whatever might lay in wait next for you.
Turn to **38**

17

The lid opens easily and you see that it is filled with a vegetable style broth. You cup your hand to taste some of the broth and find it satisfying. In fact, the broth is so delicious that you take the opportunity to consume some more until you're completely replenished. Restore 4 VITALITY points if you were previously wounded. Now if you haven't already opened them, you may look into one of the following:

The second barrel.	Turn to **32**
The third barrel.	Turn to **48**
The fourth barrel.	Turn to **65**

If you've had enough of looking into each of these barrels (or have already opened all of them), then turn to **90**

18
The climb isn't smooth and at times you feel that you are going to lose your balance, but you maintain your hold on the vine for your hands and feet to work together in order to navigate the upwards trajectory. Soon you near the highest point of the vine and with one last push, you haul yourself up and notice that the vine was securely tied to a pole in the ground. Now that you are safely on the top floor of the treetower, you stand up and take a look at your surroundings. Turn to **76**

19
The area near to the curtain is dark, but upon deciding to see what lies beyond you find that it eventually leads to a dimly lit but beautifully decorated room. The are many lavish furnishings here with another large silk curtain on the opposite wall. You convince yourself that a room of such decadence must contain some treasure, but before you can even start looking around a giant fanged serpent slithers out from behind the large curtain and makes its way towards you! This creature must be about ten metres long and as it rears its head you can make out the venom dripping out of its mouth. Transfixed with fear, you can hardly move as the serpent looks poised to bite you. Roll two dice.
If it's less than or equal to your MENTALITY, turn to **34**
If the total is greater than your MENTALITY, turn to **52**

20
Taking aim, you remove the throwing knife from your pocket and take a couple of paces back up the stairs before launching the knife at the dwarf. Roll two dice.
If the total is less than or equal to your BRUTALITY, the knife strikes the dwarf's leg which causes it to yell in pain. Turn to **66**
If the total is greater than your BRUTALITY, then you have missed. Your only option is to run up the stairs. Turn to **81**

21

Pulling the handle, the door opens and you walk into some kind of dormitory with a bunk bed up against one wall and another bunk bed directly opposite. This must be some kind of sleeping quarters for Thalkatar's guards. The only other furnishing in this room is a cupboard which is closed shut. What would you like to do?

Look at the bunk bed on the left.	Turn to **3**
Look at the bunk bed on the right.	Turn to **47**
Look inside the cupboard.	Turn to **59**
Leave the room.	Turn to **64**

22

You take hold of the vine and begin to work your way up. Feeling that you are making progress once you get halfway, you are unprepared when the vine suddenly snaps in two. You plunge down towards the ground and land awkwardly on your back. Lose 1 BRUTALITY and 2 VITALITY points. Taking some time to painfully get back up, you realise there is no other choice but to go for one of the other vines. If you haven't tried them already, which will you go for?

The middle vine.	Turn to **53**
Or the right-hand vine.	Turn to **74**

23

You decide it's not worth checking out the barrels and instead continue along the passage.
Turn to **45**

24

You take the opportunity to look behind the large curtain where the serpent crawled out from. Coming across its lair, you find a chest next to a luxurious cushion where you assume the serpent spent most of its time resting. Opening the chest, inside you find a well-crafted axe alongside some small balls of bread. You eat the bread which is very welcoming; restore 4 VITALITY points. The axe is small enough to fit inside your backpack so make a note of it on your Adventure Sheet. Satisfied that you have been well rewarded for defeating the serpent, you leave the room and head back out of the first curtain to return to your mission.
Turn to **38**

25

Raising your sword, you charge at the orc to prevent it from causing any more harm to the young man. Upon noticing you, the orc briefly stops and turns to fight you instead:

ORC
BRUTALITY 6 VITALITY 8

If you win, turn to **61**

26

Walking into the room, you see a lady sitting down at a table looking at an array of colourful magic beneath her which you realise has been causing the glow. The lady hears you enter and looks up; her face has some very deep scars.
"Hello. It is not often I encounter a previously unknown figure to enter this tower. Perhaps you would like a glimpse of the future that awaits you? Do please take a seat!" she beckons, indicating to a chair directly opposite her on the other side of the table.
If you do as the lady says, turn to **43**
If you would rather attack her, turn to **58**

27

Putting your head through the window, you look around and see nothing of interest with the exception of one tree branch happening to be hanging rather loosely compared to the other branches. You can try to snap it off should you think it could be useful.
If you do this, turn to **83**
Otherwise, you may investigate the right-hand window if you haven't already done so; in which case turn to **55**
If you've been to both windows, then the time has come to go through the central door. Turn to **89**

28

You look at the door of the tower and spot that it has a handle which no doubt will cause it to open. Turning the handle, you pull it open and a swarm of bats then fly out towards you! Roll two dice.
If it's less than or equal to our PHYSICALITY, turn to **77**
If the total is greater than your PHYSICALITY, turn to **91**

29

The flaming charcoal finds its target and a small fire breaks out on one side of Thalkatar. He flails about in agony for a short period of time before he can regain his composure and put the fire out. Severely wounded, he responds by angrily running forward towards you to attack in retaliation! You get ready and draw your sword to finish him off. Although he is already hurt, the remainder of Thalkatar's skin is still tough enough for him to sustain the loss of only 1 VITALITY point every time you manage to successfully cause damage to him with your sword:

THALKATAR
BRUTALALITY 8 PHYSICALITY 8

If you win, turn to **37**

30

You summon up your remaining strength to reach for the hilt of your sword and raise it upwards. Once it is fully drawn, you begin to hack away at the vine which causes it to loosen its hold around you but then launches a counter-attack by striking out. There is no other alternative; you must defend yourself against this vine:

VINE
BRUTALITY 7 VITALITY 6

If you win, then you manage to hack the vine into pieces where its various parts lie still on the floor and don't trouble you again. Now assuming you haven't tried either of them already, you may attempt one of the other vines:
To climb the left-hand vine, turn to **22**
To climb the middle vine, turn to **53**

31

Snapping out of your confused state, you charge up to the top of the stairs before the dwarf can ready another assault. Instead, it reaches for a warhammer next to the rocks as it prepares to do battle with you:

DWARF
BRUTALITY 7 VITALITY 8

If you win, turn to **2**

32

After opening the barrel, you take a look inside where you notice that the lower part happens to be covered with a smooth black cloth.

Do you remove the cloth to uncover what is beneath? If so, turn to **84**

Otherwise, you put the lid back on the barrel and contemplate which of the others to open if you haven't already tried them:

The first barrel.   Turn to **17**
The third barrel.   Turn to **48**
The fourth barrel.   Turn to **65**

If you've had enough of looking into each of these barrels (or have already opened all of them), then turn to **90**

33

You may have slain the ungrateful orc, but prior to that you killed an innocent young man who could have assisted you on your adventure. Feeling ashamed at what you've done, you dejectedly leave the room and walk down the next stretch of corridor.

Turn to **97**

34

You snap out of your mesmerised state just in time and leap out of the way to avoid the serpent's attack. Reaching for your sword, you get ready to fight this monstrous creature. Its tail swings as it insists on making a meal out of you for intruding in its lair:

SUPER SERPENT
BRUTALITY 8 VITALITY 10

If the serpent hits you three times, turn at once to **15**
If you win without sustaining injuries on three occasions, turn to **70**

35

The Tormentor says nothing as he looks towards you. Wearing robes made of elegant silk, his skin comprises entirely of a wooden bark as opposed to a human's flesh. Then in an instant, Thalkatar advances to where you stand. He raises his hands and you see that his fingers have been honed into long, sharp thorns which is his favoured method of attack. What weapon will you use against him?

An axe.	Turn to **46**
A slingshot.	Turn to **69**
A throwing knife.	Turn to **78**
A tinder box.	Turn to **87**
Your sword.	Turn to **93**

36

You think that the pixie might have some valuable information, so you reach down to grab it. However, the pixie despises intruders to such an extent that it is prepared to deal with unwarranted interruptions like you have just caused. The pixie casts a spell at your face which makes you lose consciousness and fall to the ground. You do not recover in time for when Thalkatar's soldiers discover you on the ground and completely immobile, which makes it easy for them to seize you. Dragged off to a horrendous fate at the hands of the Tormentor himself, your adventure ends here.

37

Thalkatar slumps to the ground, never to rise again. Thanks to your actions, the Tormentor is defeated at long last; his reign of causing trouble and misery is finally over. There certainly won't be many who will be mourning at his demise. Taking all the time you need to recover from this final battle, you reflect on what you've encountered and allow yourself a moment to savour your epic victory.
Turn to **100**

38

You come to a wall with three vines in front of it. Looking above you to see what is supporting the vines at the top, you notice they lead to another floor and that this is the only way to get to the top level of the treetower. You get ready for the ascent before deciding to choose which vine to use in order to climb upwards:

The left-hand vine.	Turn to **22**
The middle vine.	Turn to **53**
The right-hand vine.	Turn to **74**

39

The glow does not make any sense to you. Feeling that time is better spent focusing on more important matters, you conclude that whatever's producing such a shimmering light is not worth investigating. You continue down the passage.
Turn to **80**

40

You walk around the perimeter of the treetower and before finding another entrance, you instead come across a goblin supposedly on guard duty but is instead sleeping in a bricked-up archway. You tiptoe cautiously so as not to disturb it. Roll two dice.
If it's less than or equal to your MENTALITY, turn to **51**
If the total is greater than your MENTALITY, turn to **63**

41
Thankfully your reflexes are sharp and you dart backwards before the scorpion can get you. Grasping the lid, you slam it down on top of its barrel and tighten it shut so that the scorpion cannot strike again. Phew! Now assuming that hasn't put you off from opening any of the other barrels, you can open one of the following:

The first barrel.	Turn to **17**
The third barrel.	Turn to **48**
The fourth barrel.	Turn to **65**

If you've had enough of looking into each of these barrels (or have already opened all of them), then turn to **90**

42
After a short while you arrive at a door where you hear loud noises on the other side. It appears that a weapon is being used through all this commotion.
If you open the door, turn to **11**
If you disregard what may be happening, turn to **88**

43
You sit down as requested by the lady and she takes a moment to introduce herself.
"Greetings. My name is Loretta and whilst I reside in this infernal tower, that does not mean I serve Thalkatar. It was one of his former accomplices who inflicted these scars upon my face. They soon regretted their actions, for I brought an end to their life with my magic. The Tormentor has since become wary of my powers and whilst he may rule over these parts, he dare not disturb my sanctuary. Now I am willing to divulge some information that may help defeat him, but decide carefully about what you will put forward!"
You may ask Loretta one of the following three questions:

"What perils await me in the treetower?"	Turn to **7**
"How can I overcome Thalkatar himself?"	Turn to **68**
"Are there any riches here?"	Turn to **92**

44

You draw your sword and use it to cut the young man's throat, killing him instantly. The orc is taken by surprise at what you've done and then looks at you with disgust.

"Who are you?" it growls. "You've spoilt my fun – now you'll pay!" The orc raises its flail in the air at you then rushes forward to attack. You must fight:

ORC
BRUTALITY 6 VITALITY 8

If you win, turn to **33**

45

You soon come to a set of spiral stairs leading upwards that will take you to the next level of the treetower. Ascending them, you are almost at the top when rocks suddenly begin to be hurled down towards you! Avoiding the rocks, you look up to see that they are being thrown by a mischievous dwarf. Backing down to prevent yourself getting hit momentarily, what action will you take in response to the dwarf's assault?

Use a slingshot, if you have it.	Turn to **9**
Use a throwing knife, if you have it.	Turn to **20**
If you have neither, you run up the stairs.	Turn to **81**

46

You grab the axe out of your backpack. Thalkatar looks uneasy as he sees you brandish it, for this axe can cause normal damage to his skin as opposed to your conventional sword. Nonetheless he continues to advance and swinging your axe, you prepare yourself for a fight to the death:

THALKATAR
BRUTALITY 9 VITALITY 15

If you win, turn to **37**

47
Peeking at both beds, the top bunk is empty though the sheets are hiding something napping on the lower bunk.
If you pull off the sheets, turn to **71**
Otherwise, if you haven't already done so then you can do any of the following:

Look at the bunk bed on the left.	Turn to **3**
Look inside the cupboard.	Turn to **59**
Leave the room.	Turn to **64**

48
You open the barrel where an irate pixie looks up at you. "Who disturbs my slumber?" it complains. "Put the lid back down on this barrel right now! Do it or I'll make you regret having awakened me, consider this as a warning!"
If you do as the pixie instructs, turn to **10**
If you'd rather interrogate it, turn to **36**

49
Intrigued, you climb out of the window and balance yourself on the tree branches to find out what these light sources are. However, you then happen to step on a weak branch which immediately snaps in half. Losing your footing, you tumble off the remaining tree branches and plummet down on to the ground. Upon landing, you crack your skull wide open. Those beings you encountered at the top of the treetower are Will-O'-The-Wisps, who take great pleasure in luring unwitting victims to their death. Your adventure ends here.

50

You rummage through the orc's pockets and find the keys that the young man told you about. There are a few of them secured to a large ring, but after testing each of the keys you work out which of them releases the chains.

"Thank you so much!" says the man, free from his shackles. "I don't know what I would have done had you not arrived. My name is Chesley and I'm an assistant to the legendary Admiral Dunbreck – you might have heard of him! But like you I am also an adventurer who was keen to rid this treetower of Thalkatar until I was defeated and captured by that orc, who would go on to torture me for its sadistic gain. The Tormentor would occasionally come to watch but mostly left the orc to its own devices. Now that you have put an end to this vile monster, I can try to escape this tower and lead a normal life again. Alas I am too injured to assist in your personal mission, but I can at least show my gratitude by giving you something that may help to defeat Thalkatar." Chesley pulls out a tinder box that was concealed in his possession and hands it over to you.

"Wooden bark forms Thalkatar's skin", he indicates. "Should you find a branch of wood long enough and set it alight using this box, you can cause some serious damage to the Tormentor. I wish I could be there to see you do this to him. Moving on to other subjects, let us finish off some paltry scraps of poultry I was given to live off from!"

On top of a rag in a previously unseen corner of the room are some pieces of chicken which Chesley shares with you. Although these scraps are rather small, the meal is still very much welcomed by you and restores 4 VITALITY points. Then the time comes for both you and your newly gained friend to part ways. Bidding Chesley farewell, you wish him luck in his own escape. Then making a note of the tinder box on your Adventure Sheet if you haven't already done so, you proceed to head off in the opposite direction.

Turn to **97**

51

You creep stealthily forwards but the goblin does not awaken from its slumber. Breathing a sigh of relief, you proceed to continue around the treetower's perimeter but unfortunately do not find another way in. With a hint of reluctance, you conclude there seems to be only a single entrance that will get you inside. Therefore, you return there in order to gain entry into the treetower.
Turn to **28**

52

Unable to move, the serpent sinks its fangs into your neck. Lose 6 VITALITY points. If you are still alive, you summon everything you have inside you and manage to shake yourself off from being rooted to the spot. Next, you desperately reach for your sword to defend yourself from the serpent for dear life:

SUPER SERPENT
BRUTALITY 8 VITALITY 10

This is going to be a very tough fight. If the serpent wounds you again, turn at once to **8**
If somehow you win without sustaining further damage from the serpent, turn to **70**

53

You hold the vine and feel assured enough that it will do the job in helping you to climb up the wall. Taking a moment in order to get yourself focused, you then begin your ascent. Placing a firm grip on the vine with both hands, you then use your legs and feet to slowly work your way up and reach the floor located above. Roll two dice.
If it's less than or equal to your PHYSICALITY, turn to **18**
If the total is greater than your PHYSICALITY, turn to **67**

54

The dwarf is knocked back, having been unexpectedly surprised by the impact of your blow. It is dazed, but upon seeing you race up the stairs all ready for battle it makes a sharp recovery and reaches out for a warhammer next to the stack of rocks. By the time the dwarf has got hold of the warhammer, you are at the top of the stairs and keen to put an end to the suffering it has caused:

DWARF
BRUTALITY 7 VITALITY 6

If you win, turn to **2**

55

Walking up to the window, you are charmed by the sight of various glowing white balls of light that are weaving and flying their way around the tree branches. The way they move around is very captivating, though you make sure not to get too mesmerised by their presence.
If you try and get closer to whatever they may be, turn to **49**
If not, turn to **60**

56
You decide that it's best not to disturb whatever may be lurking behind the curtain. Having a sense of urgency and without wanting to waste any more time, you continue walking along the path to discover what it is that may be lying in store next.
Turn to **38**

57
You follow the passageway and eventually come across a number of barrels resting against the wall of the corridor. Their lids are all closed and you wonder if there might be anything worthwhile inside them which you could make use of further within the treetower.
If you investigate the barrels, turn to **4**
If you choose to ignore them, turn to **23**

58
Not trusting the woman, you pull out your sword but upon seeing your raised weapon the woman responds by charging her hand with a powerful spell which she then aims at you. The spell hits you in the chest, and causes you to fly backwards into the far wall with near devastating consequences. Roll one die; the number it lands on indicates the number of VITALITY points you lose due to the crushing force of this magic. If you are still alive, you see that the woman has stood up out of her chair and is looking very angrily towards you.
"Fool! How do you think I am able to survive in this wretched place against Thalkatar and his damned accomplices?" she rages. "You will receive no help from me – now begone!"
Already injured and not wanting to endure any more harm given what's just happened, you hurry out of the room before she can cast another spell against you.
Turn to **80**

59

You open up the cupboard and find it surprisingly bare save for a big green bottle filled with liquid on one of the shelves. On the bottle is a label which the word *Virtus* written on it.
If you drink the contents, turn to **16**
Otherwise, you close the cupboard and can perform one of the following actions if you haven't done so already:
Look at the bunk bed on the left. Turn to **3**
Look at the bunk bed on the right. Turn to **47**
Leave the room. Turn to **64**

60

Despite their displays of vivid radiance, you are not drawn enough by the glowing balls of light to make an attempt of getting nearer to their habitat for a much closer inspection. You turn around and decide what your next course of action should be.
There is the left-hand window which you can wander over to if you haven't been there yet, in which case turn to **27**
Or the only other option remaining is to make your way to the central door. Turn to **89**

61

The young man cheers when the orc falls at long last. Knowing that it won't be getting back up, he tells you that there are a set of keys inside one of the orc's pockets which will release him from the chains that are holding him captive.
If you search the orc's body to locate the keys, turn to **50**
If you leave the young man to fend for himself, turn to **82**

62

You fail to get yourself together, having already been struck once. Another of the dwarf's rocks comes to blows with your head, and this time the damage is severe enough to crack your skull which causes you to become completely disorientated. Losing your balance, you tumble down the stairs and have blacked out entirely when you land at the bottom. Unconscious, you are left to the mercy of Thalkatar's guards who will come across your helpless state. When they do, it is not long before you are shackled and taken to be mutilated at the hands of the Tormentor himself. Your adventure ends here.

63

Unfortunately, you kick a loose stone which then bounces along the ground and hits the goblin where it is sleeping. Immediately the creature's eyes flick open and upon seeing you, it reaches for its sword and rushes forward to attack. You must fight:

GOBLIN
BRUTALITY 5 VITALITY 6

If you win, then upon searching the goblin's body you find nothing that may be useful. You are also dismayed to learn there isn't an alternative entrance into the treetower other than the one you first came by. Ruefully, you go back to approach it.
Turn to **28**

64

The room doesn't seem to have anything worthwhile to investigate, you think to yourself. Besides, you've already come so far that Thalkatar must be nearby... surely? You press onwards.
Turn to **38**

65

Upon opening the barrel, you find that it contains a slingshot with three pebbles that you can use as ammunition. Decide whether you want to take these and if so, note them on your Adventure Sheet. Now you may open one of the following:

The first barrel.　　　　　　　　　　Turn to **17**
The second barrel.　　　　　　　　　Turn to **32**
The third barrel.　　　　　　　　　　Turn to **48**

If you've had enough of looking into each of these barrels (or have already opened all of them), then turn to **90**

66

The dwarf tries desperately to pull the knife out of its leg, but upon seeing you advance up the stairs it changes tactic and reaches for a warhammer next to the pile of rocks. By the time it has done that, you have reached the top with your sword at the ready and determined to finish off the dwarf:

DWARF
BRUTALITY 7 VITALITY 6

If you win, turn to **2**

67

You suddenly lose your grip and fall all the way back down to the stone ground, enduring a hurtful landing in the process. Lose 2 VITALITY points. Getting back up, you begin to climb the vine once more. Roll two dice again.

If the total rolled is less than or equal to your PHYSICALITY, then you may turn to **18**

If it's greater than your PHYSICALITY, you suffer an additional fall which means you lose another 2 VITALITY points. Repeat the dice-rolling process until you either successfully roll less than or equal to your PHYSICALITY, or your VITALITY drops to zero in which case you have died trying to climb the vine and your adventure ends here!

68

Her eyes light up when you decide to enquire about the Tormentor himself.

"Thalkatar's skin comprises of a wooden bark", Loretta says. "A weapon such as your sword will inflict damage upon him, but if you are to cause maximum impact then what you need is a really effective weapon such as an axe. This very weapon can be found nearby, and I hope that you do manage to get hold of it for I would most certainly delight in Thalkatar's wicked reign coming to an end. Go now, and may the very best of luck be bestowed upon you!"

You thank Loretta for the information she has provided and get up off the chair where you then leave through the door where you entered.

Turn to **80**

69

You try loading up the slingshot but this gives Thalkatar plenty of time to slash out at you, knocking the slingshot away from your hand and leaving it with a severely nasty bruise. Lose 2 VITALITY points. If you are still alive, then you hurriedly look for another weapon that could be used against the Tormentor.

If you have an axe, turn to **46**

If you use a tinder box, turn to **87**

If neither of these are available, you then draw your sword. Turn to **93**

70

You breathe a sigh of relief and take a moment to look at the serpent's decapitated remains. Knowing that it will not trouble you any longer, after a short pause you contemplate the more pressing situations further up the treetower and therefore decide what your next move will be.

If you search the room, turn to **24**

If you'd rather leave, turn to **86**

71

You rip off the bed sheets and immediately recoil in horror as you see a rotting corpse on top of the bed! Roll two dice.
If it's less than or equal to your MENTALITY, turn to **6**
If the total is greater than your MENTALITY, turn to **94**

72

The scorpion lashes out and you don't react fast enough to avoid being struck by its tail. Your arm is badly affected by the scorpion's poison, causing the loss of 1 BRUTALITY and 4 VITALITY points. If you're still alive, then the scorpion's attack has left you shaken. Not wanting to look in any more barrels after this encounter, the alternative option for you is to escape out of here and run down the corridor. Turn to **45**

73

Making it all the way to the top of the spiralling stairs safely, you unsheathe your sword and get ready to fight the dwarf to the death. The dwarf responds by reaching for a warhammer next to its pile of rocks then begins to advance. Let the battle commence:

DWARF
BRUTALITY 7 VITALITY 8

If you win, turn to **2**

74

You put your hand on the vine and consider whether it will be strong enough to hold your weight. As you are doing this however, the vine suddenly comes to life and begins to encircle itself around your body! Desperately, you reach for your sword in order to cut the vine's hold. Roll two dice.
If it's less than or equal to your MENTALITY, turn to **30**
If the total is greater than your MENTALITY, turn to **99**

75
Your aim misses and the flame on the charcoal is extinguished. There is no time to use the tinder box again as Thalkatar is almost upon you! All that is left for you to do is draw your sword.
Turn to **93**

76
You look around and take a moment to recognise what gives the treetower its very name. Two windows are situated either side of you but neither contain any glass. Instead, they are covered with leaves and tree branches with a few of the latter growing inwards towards the floor and ceiling of the tower. Ahead of you is a large wood-panelled door which no doubt leads to Thalkatar himself. Do you feel confident enough to challenge the Tormentor, or would you rather look through the windows first?
If you take a look at the left-hand window, turn to **27**
If you would like to see what's at the right-hand window, turn to **55**
If you head straight for the wooden door, turn to **89**

77

You duck out of the way and the bats fly harmlessly above your head. They do not return to attack, which means you are free to enter the treetower without the threat of any further obstruction.

Turn to **14**

78

Hurling the knife at Thalkatar, you then watch in disbelief as he raises one of his hands to catch it. The knife lands in his hands but because of the Tormentor's wooden-like skin it causes no damage. As Thalkatar pulls out the knife and disposes of it, you desperately try to come up with an alternative course of action.

If you have an axe, turn to **46**
If you use a tinder box, turn to **87**
If neither of these are available, you then draw your sword. Turn to **93**

79

The second level of the treetower looks virtually similar as the first, with passageways once again leading off to the left and right. There doesn't seem to be a particular indication of which path is the best to proceed along, and therefore it's ultimately your decision as to which route you believe to be the best one to take.

If you head left, turn to **13**
If you head right, turn to **42**

80

You soon come to another doorway with a rich, elegant silk curtain hanging over the way in. There is no way of seeing what lies beyond the curtain, nor can you hear anything from the other side.

If you pull back the curtain, turn to **19**
If you disregard it and walk past, turn to **56**

81

Rushing upwards in a zig-zag manoeuvre to minimise the chances of you getting struck, you race up the stairs whilst the dwarf relentlessly pelts rocks down at you. Roll two dice.
If it's less than or equal to your PHYSICALITY, turn to **73**
If the total is greater than your PHYSICALITY, turn to **95**

82

Not wanting to engage with the young man, you dash out of the door to let him find the keys for himself. The orc is dead and the young man doesn't appear to be restrained too much; with this in mind you continue on your way to find out what's lying beyond.
Turn to **97**

83

You position yourself on the ledge to pull away at the branch. It takes a bit of vigorous yanking and twisting but after a few minutes your patience is rewarded with it at long last breaking off. Slowly bringing it forward, you discover that upon closer inspection the branch is revealed to be some two metres in length. Pleased with this acquired gain, you carry it with you.
Now if you haven't already done so, you can choose to go over to the right-hand window in which case turn to **55**
Otherwise, you acknowledge that you must go through the central door. Turn to **89**

84

You lift up the cloth and are horrified to find a massive scorpion lurking underneath it! Upon seeing you, the scorpion raises its poisonous tail and gets ready to strike. Roll two dice.
If it's less than or equal to your PHYSICALITY, turn to **41**
If the total is greater than your PHYSICALITY, turn to **72**

85

The passage is long and winding as you follow it for some distance. Eventually there is the sound of footsteps, and then you catch a glimpse of someone approaching towards you. But this creature is by no means friendly as it is a troll sent out by Thalkatar to investigate the commotion on the lower floor of the treetower. Upon seeing you, the troll rushes forward with its weapon at the ready. You must fight it:

TROLL
BRUTALITY 6 VITALITY 6

If you win, turn to **96**

86

Your ordeal against the serpent has been so exhausting that you can't wait to get out of this room and leave it behind. Once you are past the curtain and out of the doorway, you refocus on completing what you set out to do originally.
Turn to **38**

87

You remove a flint, steel and a stick of charcoal from the tinder box before Thalkatar can seize an opportunity to attack. Striking them together, you are fortunate to create a spark of flame at the first attempt. As the charcoal starts to burn red, do you have a bigger item that you can ignite?
If you are carrying a tree branch, turn to **5**
If not, turn to **98**

88

You decide that whatever's happening on the other side of the door is none of your concern, so you leave it be and continue onwards to deal with your own pressing matters.
Turn to **97**

89

Bringing yourself together, you cautiously step up to the large wood panelled door and push it open. It is not locked, but the very moment after walking through you find yourself plunged into darkness. For a moment you're uncertain of what could possibly be happening, then all of a sudden there is a scintillating flash and the room you are in is filled with a flickering light. Flaming torches are now burning on the opposite wall... and in between them is none other than Thalkatar himself!
Turn to **35**

90

Leaving the barrels behind, you decide to continue your journey down the passageway in order to find out what else is in wait ahead.
Turn to **45**

91

You are caught in the middle as the bats flap their wings past you. In a moment of confusion this causes you to lose your balance and sharply fall to the ground rather awkwardly. Lose 2 VITALITY points. Staying on the ground afterwards, you hold on until you are certain that all of the bats have flown away before carefully picking yourself up and dusting off your garments. Taking a cautious look around to ensure there aren't any more unexpected surprises which are set to come out of nowhere, once satisfied that the coast is clear you finally enter the treetower.
Turn to **14**

92

Loretta sighs after hearing your enquiry, and with a reluctant shake of the head seems a bit reluctant to assist.

"If it's riches you're after, then prepare to be extremely disappointed!" she says in a more lowered tone. "Honestly, I was hoping that you would ask me something more interesting. For alas, the only reward you'll receive for defeating Thalkatar is reputation. No items of sentimental value can be found within this tower."

You acknowledge Loretta's response and decide not to bother her any further. Standing out of the chair, you then leave through the same door where you came in.

Turn to **80**

93

With your sword drawn and ready to fight, you feel determined to prove to Thalkatar that you are not daunted by what looks set to be a final showdown in this treetower. However, due to the nature of the Tormentor's tough skin, your usually reliable weapon will not be as effective in damaging him compared to other opponents you have previously faced off against. Each time you successfully land a hit on him, Thalkatar will only lose 1 VITALITY point. The Tormentor closes in on you with his hands raised, poised to lash out and convinced that he has the initiative. You defend yourself as this very enduring battle gets underway:

THALKATAR
BRUTALITY 9 VITALITY 15

If you win defying all the odds, turn to **37**

94

The horrific appearance of the corpse grips you with fear. You will not be able to shake this from your memory for an extremely long time to come, and the sight is so revolting that it ends up creating a major impact on your judgment. Lose 1 BRUTALITY and 1 PHYSICALITY point. Stepping back in disgust, you move as far away as you can from this hideous atrocity. Eventually it comes to a point where you're so distant that you've actually backed out of the room and after taking a moment to compose yourself, attention turns to continuing down the passage again.
Turn to **38**

95

One of the rocks thrown by the dwarf is a direct hit, whacking you firmly on the head. Lose 2 VITALITY points. The force of this blow makes you somewhat dizzy, with everything around you feeling like it is almost a blur. Desperately trying to recover from the wound you've just sustained, you do everything possible to get back on track. Roll two dice.
If it's less than or equal to your MENTALITY, turn to **31**
If the total is greater than your MENTALITY, turn to **62**

96

The troll's lifeless body falls to the ground. You search it and find a throwing knife as well as a fresh block of cheese. Whilst this was unlikely to be one of the most difficult fights you've had as a warrior, the cheese is nonetheless very welcome in getting your energy levels back up once again. Restore 4 VITALITY points. Afterwards, you examine the knife and decide that it could be useful later on, so place it inside your pocket securely. Note down the knife on your Adventure Sheet. Satisfied with your gains from the troll, you continue onwards.
Turn to **45**

97

Another door soon appears. Walking up to it, you find that it is closed firmly shut and upon leaning on the door with your ear alert for potential noises, do not hear any sounds being made on the other side.

If you open the door, turn to **21**

If you would rather not investigate what could be within, turn to **64**

98

You throw the stick of charcoal in the hope that it can do some significant damage to the opponent you are currently up against. Roll two dice.

If it's less than or equal to your PHYSICALITY, turn to **29**

If the total is greater than your PHYSICALITY, turn to **75**

99

The vine has secured a firm grip on you. Unable to move, the only thing you can do is watch in squealing horror as it proceeds to crawl up your body then wraps itself around your neck to strangle you of all the remaining life force you have. Your adventure ends here.

100

As you leave where you are behind and make your way back down the treetower, your thoughts turn to the good people of Falconleas Wood in regards to how you'll be telling them the good news of Thalkatar's permanent demise. If you happened to meet Loretta at some point during your adventure, you make sure of returning to her and proudly stating that the Tormentor is finally dead; she can live her remaining days in peace without having to suffer from his unwanted interference. You rightfully deserve every positive accolade that shall be granted to you as a result of this successful mission which is already being regarded as one of the most triumphant of days. Congratulations.

Tormentor Treetower

EPILOGUE

If you've made it this far, then here's a bonus part of the book especially for you. I thought I would conclude proceedings by offering some insight into the processes that went towards my planning as well as how all the included adventures came to existence.

I chose the name Quadportal for the title as quad in Latin means four – as you might have guessed, four adventures and each adventure is a portal to a location where you are the main character who makes the necessary decisions. The reasoning for capping all of the adventures at 100 sections each is that so they can easily be played within a short space of time. It also allows me to find out which particular adventures work better should I happen write a larger individual gamebook in the future based on a similar setting.

In writing each adventure, it gave me the opportunity to experiment with various environments that usually make for common scenarios in gamebook adventures that are based within the realms of fantasy.

Ripper Reaperman forms the testing ground as to how exploring an open world landscape might possibly work, and keeping it largely within a town centre meant I could also confine the adventure to my set limit of 100 sections. Much of it was influenced by the electronic music acts KnifeLadder and Black Light Ascension; incidentally two of the former's members currently make up BLA! Nods towards both acts in terms of personnel, album/song titles and other obscure references can be found throughout the adventure – if you want to hear what they sound like for yourself, then by all means do check out:
knifeladder.bandcamp.com
blacklightascension.bandcamp.com

Ultraviolator Underworld was actually the first adventure I commenced work on, but also the very last of the included four to be written in full. I had mapped out everything that needed to be done and afterwards began writing the adventure, but for whatever reason I stopped work on it and went on to write the other three featured adventures instead. This would actually go on to result in my favour, as during the summer of 2023 I spent a weekend in North Wales with the lovely Emma Owen. We visited one particular spot that gave me ideas on how to resurrect this particular adventure, such as changing the setting from a dank sewer to a network of cavernous mines. The title was also revised to what it is now; given that I wrote the other three adventures in between starting and finishing this one you may have noticed a slight change in writing style as I developed and honed my technique whilst penning each of them.

Spiritual Sacrilege has its themes set mainly thanks to the legendary TV series GamesMaster, though to be more specific the location and theme of the first series. I liked the idea of situating an adventure inside a gothic religious building, as well as interacting with a number of holy (and unholy) characters. Listening to a soundtrack of chants by the Cistercian Monks provided the optimal background music! The name of Kethnick was conceived whilst thinking about the artist Nick Spender, who did the internal illustrations for Fighting Fantasy gamebook The Rings of Kether. Coincidentally I came up with this antagonist's name *before* Nick sadly passed away in January 2024. Another Fighting Fantasy gamebook, Dead of Night, was the basis for some of the other characters who make an appearance in this adventure. Father Bambrand is an amalgamation of this epic book's two writers Jim Bambra and Stephen Hand, Brother Oakry is a nod towards cover artist Terry Oakes and Abbot Markenna is my way of paying tribute to its interior illustrator – the late, great, Martin McKenna.

Tormentor Treetower claims the distinction of being the very first of all these adventures I managed to fully complete writing for. Once it had passed some thorough playtesting and proofreading, it was then given away as a free PDF in the summer of 2023 though I did also do a very small number of printed copies in booklet form. The main purpose for going ahead with the latter was to see for myself what a printed copy of my work would look like, and as well as keeping one of these copies for myself I gave a copy each to my mum and sister in addition to certain members of the gamebook community who have become some of my closest friends over these years. Introducing everyone to a sample of my work also provided an opportunity to receive feedback in order to improve both this adventure and any others that I would go on to write. One of the recommended suggestions was to alter a couple of characteristic names to what they are known as now within this book. When it came to writing this adventure itself, I felt it to be of some importance that something simple would be the best method of hitting the ground running. So I decided that by equally splitting 100 sections over three levels as best as I could, this would result in about thirty sections per level with an additional scene prior to entering the treetower (hence the encounter with a sleeping goblin outside). As soon as the adventurer finds themselves in the treetower, they get to meet as well as on some occasions do battle with creatures one can almost guarantee to find somewhere in your standard fantasy adventure gamebook. The notable exception to this of course is the main bad guy Thalkatar, who I perceived as a silent but deranged woodland folk. Although what's indeed similar to the other adventures I wrote is by myself having some particular music to help shape how everything was developed. On this occasion it was the American band Pavement whose tunes would weave their magic into the look and feel of what happens within the treetower, hence the reference to them in certain aspects of the adventure.

I would also like to give an extremely worthy mention to both Matthew Dewhurst and Waclaw Traier, whose illustrations feature throughout what you've been reading.

Matthew did the front-page art for Tormentor Treetower and I was very impressed by what he produced from the brief provided by myself that I decided to commission him again for the front-page illustrations that would be used at the beginning of the other adventures. Hence Matthew also went on to do Spiritual Sacrilege, Ripper Reaperman and Ultraviolator Underworld (in that order).

Waclaw originally did the cover art for another gamebook, but alas the decision was taken that it would not be used. However, after some time spent admiring the potential of this cover I decided to purchase both the license for it as well as the original artwork – unquestionably I'm very glad to have felt that justice has been done by choosing this art as the wraparound cover for my own gamebook. Various filler illustrations have additionally made their way into this book throughout and these were provided by Waclaw too; most of them can be found in the Grim Freaks Art Asset Pack which can be purchased from his website **droned.eu**.

Again, a massive thanks to Matthew and Waclaw for how they've helped to visualise this book.

WHAT NEXT?

I certainly hope to write more adventure gamebooks in the years ahead. Hopefully what's featured this particular book will have given some taste. There'll definitely be consideration for adventures lasting over a hundred sections.

I'm currently exploring the idea of a mental health-themed gamebook; there's been times over the years where I've struggled with all the related symptoms and nowadays when it's possible, I strive to be a passionate advocate on everything relating to the subject of mental health as it's important to share experiences and offer support.

I've also got ideas lined up for developing my own gamebook series. With optimism creeping in, there's something within me which is saying there's plenty of years ahead. As time goes by, I'll be feeling confident enough to be writing adventures that others will enjoy playing. This also includes promoting the works of my fellow gamebook authors (some of who are mentioned on the next page).

I would also like to encourage others by stating that *you* also have the ability to write something within yourself, and it doesn't have to be a gamebook adventure. Of course, it's worth pointing out that everything doesn't happen overnight – in my case it did take a year to put this book together. Believe in me when I say that by giving yourself time and patience, eventually you will succeed.

If you would like to get in touch anytime, by all means do drop me an e-mail at jimthegamebookwriter@gmail.com.

Thanks for reading my words.

James Aukett

OTHER GAMEBOOK SERIES THAT MAY BE OF INTEREST

Ace Gamebooks by Jonathan Green:
facebook.com/ACEgamebooks

Destiny's Role by Mark Lain:
facebook.com/DestinysRole

Literally Immersive Gamebooks by James A Hirons:
jamsplace.co

Savage Realms Gamebooks by TroyAnthony Schermer:
tinyurl.com/SavageRealmsGamebooks

RIPPER REAPERMAN

CHARACTERISTICS

BRUTALITY
Starting Brutality =

PHYSICALITY
Starting Physicality =

MENTALITY
Starting Mentality =

VITALITY
Starting Vitality =

BATTLE ENCOUNTERS

Brutality =
Vitality =

Brutality =
Vitality =

Brutality =
Vitality =

Brutality =
Vitality =

Brutality =
Vitality =

Brutality =
Vitality =

ADVENTURE SHEET

ITEMS CARRIED

FOOD PARCELS

| 3 | 2 | 1 | 0 |

NOTES

ULTRAVIOLATOR UNDERWORLD

CHARACTERISTICS

BRUTALITY
Starting
Brutality =

VITALITY
Starting
Vitality =

PHYSICALITY
Starting
Physicality =

MENTALITY
Starting
Mentality =

BATTLE ENCOUNTERS

Brutality =
Vitality =

Brutality =
Vitality =

Brutality =
Vitality =

Brutality =
Vitality =

Brutality =
Vitality =

Brutality =
Vitality =

ADVENTURE SHEET

ITEMS CARRIED

FOOD PARCELS

| 3 | 2 | 1 | 0 |

NOTES

SPIRITUAL SACRILEGE

CHARACTERISTICS

BRUTALITY
Starting Brutality =

PHYSICALITY
Starting Physicality =

MENTALITY
Starting Mentality =

VITALITY
Starting Vitality =

BATTLE ENCOUNTERS

Brutality = Vitality =	Brutality = Vitality =
Brutality = Vitality =	Brutality = Vitality =
Brutality = Vitality =	Brutality = Vitality =

ADVENTURE SHEET

ITEMS CARRIED

FOOD PARCELS

| 3 | 2 | 1 | 0 |

NOTES

TORMENTOR TREETOWER

CHARACTERISTICS

BRUTALITY
Starting Brutality =

PHYSICALITY
Starting Physicality =

MENTALITY
Starting Mentality =

VITALITY
Starting Vitality =

BATTLE ENCOUNTERS

Brutality =
Vitality =

Brutality =
Vitality =

Brutality =
Vitality =

Brutality =
Vitality =

Brutality =
Vitality =

Brutality =
Vitality =

ADVENTURE SHEET

ITEMS CARRIED

FOOD PARCELS

| 3 | 2 | 1 | 0 |

NOTES